SUGAR DADDY'S GAME

Sugar Daddy's Game

A NOVEL BY

GREGORY D. DIXON

Q-Boro Books
WWW.QBOROBOOKS.COM

An Urban Entertainment Company

Dedication

This is dedicated to my daughters Katina, Tara, Andrea, and AnnElisha.
I will always be your Sugar Daddy!

Acknowledgments

First and foremost, this book could not have been written without the support, encouragement, faith, love, and the gentle prodding of my friend, sister, and number-one fan. To my Editorial Liaison/Agent, Linda Williams. Thank you, darling; you're one in a million. Thanks to Mark Anthony and Carl Weber and their whole organization for the chance. Peace.

SUGAR DADDY'S GAME

PROLOGUE

Elnora was scared. She huddled in a corner of the living room and listened as the men outside pounded on the front door. This was her fault. She had left the burglar bars unlatched because Sugar's women would be starting to come through soon. Now they would both pay.

Trembling in fear and awash in guilt, she called his name. "Sugar! Please. They're almost in!"

The front door was set in a steel frame. This was the only reason the men weren't in yet. With the house so far back from the street, and the stone wall surrounding it on three sides, the chances of someone hearing and calling for help were nil. She dare not call the cops herself. Sugar had said not to.

"Open the fuckin' door, nigga! We know you an' that bitch in there! You fucked over the wrong one this time."

She could hear the muffled shouts as the men took turns kicking the solid wood. Nora jumped when she heard the first *crack!* as the door finally started to give under the assault. She jumped again, and gave a little squeal as a shadow moved across her huddled form. The sound turned into a sigh of relief as she realized who it was.

"Sugar."

The man standing before her laid the big pistol in his hand on the mantle over the fireplace. He reached a hand down to her where she crouched. "Nora. Come on, baby. It's going to be all right. I'll take care of it. I promise."

As he pulled her up and into his arms, she leaned into him during the momentary silence. The top of her head barely reached the center of his chest, but it wasn't his size that made her feel safe. It was him. He'd always kept her safe. People had often wondered why she wore those long, shapeless dresses. Her hair was always pulled up into a severe bun. No makeup and those big, ugly glasses. Not Sugar, though. He knew. And he knew his touch was the only one she could stand. And that only barely. Even now, after all this time, Sugar held her until the shaking stopped. He kept his eyes on the door, though, even with the adrenaline rush and soft tension of Nora's breasts against his chest. He felt the smoothness of her back and her hips through the heavy cloth.

Yes, he knew why she had retreated from all feelings, especially physical ones. They had lived together in this house for over two years, yet had barely touched. Still, he remembered the brown perfection of her body's silhouette through a backlit nightgown. Especially, he remembered how beautiful she was when she had allowed herself to be a woman.

Right now, though, he had bigger problems to deal with. Now that Nora was calmer, he gently led her to the stairs. "Go to your room. Lock the door and don't come out until I tell you. Now."

Gone was the gentle Sugar who'd soothed her fears. Looking up into his eyes, she saw the man who had saved her when she was about to die. Somehow this made her fear abate. Gathering her skirts, she ran up the stairs without another word.

Sugar strode quickly back to the fireplace. Pushing down hard on the sides of the metal basket holding the utensils, he twisted it to the right. There was a click. He pushed on the bricks to the right of the mantle, and a five-foot section of the wall swung inward. Ducking through the opening into a small room, he hit a switch. A low-wattage bulb came on.

"Shit."

He'd forgotten his gun. Ducking back through the wall, he retrieved the pistol and went back into the room. A table held a metal strongbox. The only other items in the cubbyhole were his weapons. He quickly put the pistol on the shelf and grabbed a twelve-gauge pump shotgun. Making sure the clip was full, he worked the action and chambered a round.

Reentering the living room, he killed the lamp and moved over against the wall to the left of the door. The thuds and grunts from the other side had resumed. One of the heavy oak panels in the center of the door had cracked. He could see the scar in the wood by the light seeping through the fan-shaped glass at the door's top.

Making as little noise as possible, he went over and released the half-inch deadbolts at the top and bottom of the door. Now only the lock in the center secured it. The wait wasn't long.

Two loud explosions showered splinters into the room, and holes appeared in the door panel near the lock. The men outside had grown impatient. A few more thuds, and a three-inch ragged hole let light from outside bleed into the room. Sugar didn't move. The hole darkened as a gloved hand came in and fumbled with the latch.

With a click, the door unlocked. Suddenly, it swung open violently and crashed against the stop. Two men in dark clothes and hoods rushed in. One held a long gun of some sort, and the other a pistol. Sugar stayed silent against the wall.

"I can't see shit in here. Where the fuck are they?"

"Probably upstairs. He's a weak trick. Should be no problem. Don't shoot the bitch, though. I want to see what's under that ugly shit she wears all the time."

Sugar spoke softly. "Hey."

The man closest to him, the one with the assault rifle, turned around.

BOOM!

The shotgun blast ripped into him and threw him against the stair rail. The fraction of a second's hesitation and the fact that the man with the handgun looked at his companion's body first were all that Sugar needed.

BOOM!

The shotgun spoke again. The man's head seemed to disintegrate. Blood and brain matter flew everywhere.

In the sudden quiet, Sugar let out his breath. Stepping around the mess, he moved to the side of the stairs.

"Nora!" He heard her door open. "Don't come down. Get your cell phone and call 911. Say you heard gunshots. Stay in your room until I come."

Sugar walked out the door. Going around the house, he went into the garage and grabbed his extension ladder. Placing it against the side of the house, he used his pocket knife to cut the telephone wires. Leaving the ladder, he went back inside long enough to leave the shotgun by the door and to make sure the hidden room was locked. Then he went back outside to wait for the police.

Nora huddled against the wall next to the dresser in her upstairs bedroom. Her small body trembled from head to toe in fear. Panic made chaos of her thoughts.

Dimly, she heard the booming sounds from downstairs as the men tried to force their way into the house.

They're going to kill him! she thought. *Sugar can't stop them. Then they'll come for me, just like before.*

Unbidden, her mind went back to the day, as a teenager, when her whole life changed. Images flashed across her mind. Abu. The feel of the cold steel of the knife cutting her flesh.

Hands everywhere, ripping at her clothes and her body. Pain. Oceans of it. In her ass. Her pussy. Her face as they beat her. Mind-numbing terror, until she broke inside.

The terror had never really left her. Not even after all these years. Now it was happening again. Men wanted to rape, hurt, and humiliate her. They wanted to kill Sugar.

The gunshots made her jump and emit a sharp scream. Before the first *boom* of the shotgun, she had crawled to the front of the dresser and opened the bottom drawer. The pistol Sugar had given her lay there, wrapped in the oily rag. He had taught her and all the girls to shoot, something he'd forced Nora to participate in.

By the time her shaking fingers had inserted the clip and loaded a round into the chamber, she heard the first shotgun blast. The second came as she rushed toward the door. Then she heard his voice.

"Nora."

She opened the door, the gun held across her chest.

"Don't come down. Get your cell phone and call 911. Say you heard gunshots. Stay in your room until I come."

Nora closed the door and sank to her knees. This time her body shook with gratitude. The tears were now tears of joy. She was glad that Sugar was alive. He'd taken care of the men who wanted to hurt her just as he had promised. Once again he'd saved her.

Also, her joy stemmed from the fact that she hadn't had to go downstairs into the gunfire. A burst of wonder struck her as she realized just what she had been about to do. In spite of her fear—if literally being scared shitless—she had been on her way to help Sugar.

For the first time in years she had made a conscious choice to step out from the wall of indifference and invisibility she had built around herself. There was no way to escape the inevitable conclusion: Sugar meant that much to her.

Even while following his instructions and calling the police, Nora was trying to come to terms with her new mental state. Years of hiding in the background, of exiting only to be Sugar's shadow, weren't going to go away overnight.

All of Sugar's efforts, that of the girls, the counselors they made her go to—none of it had worked. Now, something inside her had shifted again. She reached a decision. For now, she would do nothing. Everything would stay the same while she dealt with the nightmares and fears about what had happened to her.

Now, she knew she could do it. What she was more unsure of was what she could do about the way she really felt about Sugar. And about the The Game. She put away the gun and lay back on the bed, lost in thought.

CHAPTER ONE

Two Weeks Earlier . . .

In the chilly air just before dawn, Sugar banked his fires. The long row of barbecue pits threw off a wave of heat that made the air in their vicinity hot. Closing the lids of all six pits, he walked into the rear of his restaurant.

"Pits will be ready in a minute, Nora. Need any help?"

"No, thank you. The meat's almost done."

Sugar looked over at his partner and housemate. She was short, only just over five feet tall, and her overall appearance now, and whenever she was in public, was unattractive. That suited her just fine, he knew. Her hair was pulled back into an old-fashioned school teacher's bun, and her dress was a shapeless sack.

Like most things in life though, especially people, Nora was not all she appeared. Sugar remembered this. He could never forget it. Whenever he looked at her, his thoughts returned to the first time he'd seen her. It was also the last time he'd killed someone. He remembered the caramel perfection of her skin. The perfect breasts and round ass. The almost Oriental aspect of her beauty. He also remembered the blood.

Shaking his head to dispel the memories, he moved to help her work the seasoning into the meat; the huge, trimmed beef briskets, the thick steaks, plump chickens, sausage links, shark steaks, giant shrimp, and flounder.

"The slaw is in the ice box, the beans are done, and the corn is ready for the grill." Nora never really met his eyes as she talked. This, along with the way she dressed, was another consequence of her past.

"Sugar's Bar-B-Q" sat on a lot three blocks outside of Gate Seven of the Air Force base, just off Howard Avenue. Huge signs at either end of a thirty-foot-long, fifteen-foot-deep aluminum and cinder block building announced the hours of operation. The menu never changed. The food was excellent, and the business a surprising success.

Last year, he cleared over ninety thousand dollars after expenses and salaries, which included one thousand dollars a week for both him and Elnora. He'd never expected this. Not in less than two years. He was now at a point where he could shut The Game down, if he wished.

He didn't want to, though. While he no longer needed the money, the hustle excited him. The con was airtight, the marks clueless, and the pussy plentiful and first-rate. It was extremely dangerous, too, but that was only added spice. It was his—Sugar's Game.

As if reading his thoughts, Nora asked, "Who's on for tonight?"

"Mary, Taneesha, then Jessica."

She nodded. Tonight, back at the house, she would, as always, direct traffic and watch his back, unnoticed and in the shadows. He would never know how much she hated The Game, despite the fact that he gave her a generous share of the profits, like he did from the restaurant.

They worked side by side to prepare the meat and seafood, some of which had been marinating overnight, onto a big, wheeled trolley. At this time of morning, there was only the two of them in the huge kitchen. Mack, who helped Sugar work the pits, would be in soon.

Once the meat started cooking, Nora would work out front, overseeing the waitresses and cashiers. The original plan in locating so close to the Air Force base was to make the thousands of military and civilian employees their chief source of income. Sugar's unique and secret sauce was the key.

What they hadn't really counted on was how fast word would spread up and down the coast. Casino employees and patrons, strippers and hookers from the many clubs, fishermen, shipyard workers, and regular travelers on nearby Highway 90 all flocked to, or ordered from, Sugar's. They had expanded this building and the number of pits twice. Now, a couple of venture capitalists were offering huge sums to Sugar for his place, or urging him to franchise.

He had continued to avoid making a decision. Even though The Game was not, and never had been, about the money (he wasn't a fucking pimp, for Christ's sake), it generated large sums.

All his life, he'd had nothing. He'd been nothing. A whore's son from the wrong side of the tracks. The taunts and comments stopped when he learned to fight.

He and his best friend Cole walked the streets of the roughest part of a rough town with impunity. Niggas knew better than to fuck with either of them. They and the girls had become family. Sugar had not only been accepted, but was generally acknowledged as their leader.

Still, he could see it in some of the local people's eyes, could read their thoughts:

That li'l nigga Sugar and them hoodlums he runs with ain't never gon' amount to nothing. No wonder. They jus' a bunch of prostitutes' li'l bastards.

He hated that look! Hated imagining those hateful words. Well, he'd shown them. This place was totally legit, built by his and Nora's hard work and sacrifice.

Common sense dictated that he take the money offered for his business. He and Nora would never have to work again. Cole and the girls—his family—would be set too. Naturally he would break them off, and they could all do whatever they wanted to.

The truth was, he really, really enjoyed the look on those locals' faces when they came in and saw his name in the huge letters all over the place. He enjoyed the way they frowned when the cash registers rang like clockwork.

This old "whore's son" had made it big, and he really enjoyed rubbing their noses in it. On the real, though, he knew this petty revenge wasn't a good enough reason to pass up the offer of a lifetime.

He would have to get everybody together, including Cole, and talk about it. Of course, they would say, "It's up to you, Sugar. It's your place."

Then he'd go left on them, cuss 'em out, and they would all get down to the business of deciding what to do. And he would make Nora participate, even if he had to light a fire under her pretty little ass.

He smiled at the thought of all the people he loved most in the world being together and kicking it like the old days. Looking at his watch, Sugar realized it was time to get back to work.

By ten o'clock, the early rush was in full swing. A shiny white Lexus pulled into the parking lot. Heads turned as a beautiful young woman in a white leather skirt and vest got out and walked briskly inside Sugar's. Before she even made it to the counter, Sugar stepped in from the back.

Ignoring Nora, the woman walked up to Sugar.

"Hi, baby. I need two plates with shrimp, slaw, and fries. To go."

As Sugar nodded to Nora, the woman lifted a section of the countertop and came through. Standing close to Sugar, she smiled.

"It will probably be late when I come. Is that okay?"

"Sure, Jess." He smiled back, and as Nora sat the trays on the counter next to them, he reached into his pocket and pulled out a wad of bills. Peeling off a fifty, he handed it to Jessica.

Watching her ass twitch all the way back to her car, one of the customers at a nearby table said to his companion, "Now that's the shit. Bitch looks so good, the man pays her to order his food."

"Why do you think they call him 'Sugar'? He's a Sugar Daddy to a lot of hoes. Hell, I'd be her daddy anytime."

"If you wan' to die. Tha's Jessica Delano, Bullet's woman. Sugar can smile and give her money, but if ol' Sugar thinks he's gonna fuck her, he's dead meat."

The two men laughed and continued to eat.

Sugar suppressed a smile as he turned to go back to the pits. He'd overheard. They were wrong on both counts. How he'd got his name, and whether or not he was fucking Jessica. That was the beauty of The Game.

Jessica smiled as she got into her Lexus and placed the food on the passenger seat. Although she hadn't even turned her head to look, she could feel the eyes of every man in the restaurant on her ass as she walked away.

She had deliberately put some extra sway in her hips,

hoping one of the lecherous bastards would skeet down their pants legs while imagining her fucking his brains out.

Her smile faltered as she wondered if Sugar was watching too. It's not like he had to. The Game was on for tonight. For the thousandth time she wondered just how much of it was a game for her and how much was for real.

"Don't go there, Jess. You know that's not part of the deal. And you're the one who started it."

Suddenly she laughed out loud. It was that ludicrous.

"Nigga's got me talking to myself," she muttered.

Changing gears, she thought about Bullet. Now that was really worth a smile. She'd go home, watch him pig out on the food she brought, then play her own private game with him.

She would give him the fifty she got from Sugar, and listen as he commented on how her old childhood friend was a trick and a limp-dicked sugar daddy. He'd pocket the money, never quite snapping to the fact that later on he would give that back and more.

Then she would probably have to fuck him.

"Yuck," she said aloud.

Her thoughts wandered to Cole as she drove. If there was ever a man she could give all of herself to, other than Sugar, it would be him. When they were all young, looking out for each other in the hell that was their lives, it was a kind of unofficial rule that they didn't fuck each other.

Jessica was pretty sure that Cole and Taneesha broke that rule. She remembered being more than a little jealous. This was right before Cole had to leave and the rule went out the window anyway.

Sometimes she thought that she would trade all the money, the car, clothes, bling, and other fine things she now had for the way things used to be for them all. When they were all together, the world couldn't touch them.

But Cole had to leave and there was only Sugar. Sugar, he raised such conflicted emotions in her. That's why she played—needed to keep playing—The Game. Right now, though, she had Bullet to deal with.

CHAPTER TWO

"Ungh! Ungh! Aaah!" Bullet groaned as he spent himself inside Jessica's body.

She lay beneath him, legs spread wide, and mentally evaluated the quality of her acting during her faked orgasm. On a scale of one to ten, she gave it an eight. Mercifully it was brief. So was Bullet. As he rose from her and the bed, she studied him.

Dark-skinned, well-built, reasonably good-looking, and wallowing in cash, he should have been a dream man. Especially with her background. In a moment of brutal honesty, she reflected on why he wasn't. Partly, it was her. She already knew who her dream man was, and Bullet couldn't touch him. The other reason was that Bullet was a selfish asshole.

She was a trophy to him. He showered her with money, bought her nice clothes and things, and this house in which they lived, off Lamey Bridge Road in North Biloxi, was practically a mansion. But of himself, he gave nothing. She now knew that was because there was nothing to give.

His being the biggest mid-level drug dealer on the coast had nothing to do with it. Look at her dream man. Even with his sordid background, he had made something of himself. Also, he was the most caring, considerate, and giving man she had ever known. And speaking of giving.

"Say, baby, is it okay if me, M.J., and Lana go to New Orleans to shop today?"

Bullet, having washed up, was getting dressed. Jessica could see that his mind was already on his business. Even if she stayed home, he wouldn't be back until well after midnight.

"I got a lot of shit to do, anyway. Them niggas over off Division ain't coming correct with my paper. An' I got to go see Cisco. Go 'head, ma."

He walked to his nightstand and pulled a big wad of bills from his drawer. Throwing it on the bed, he grabbed his keys and cell phone. "Buy something for Daddy too." Without a backward glance, let alone a caress, he left.

Sighing, Jessica rose from the bed and went to the bathroom to bathe. Turning from the tub, she caught sight of herself in the full-length mirror on the door. Light brown skin, classic features, and long hair, she saw a very good-looking woman reflected. Her breasts were large and upright. The thatch of pubic hair was thick and well-trimmed. Legs to die for. She could find very little physical fault.

Men paid attention wherever she went. Few took it too far because it was known that she was Bullet's woman. So no one knew just how miserable she was. She had never felt this bad about herself. Not even when she was a teenager turning tricks.

"I know what you need," she whispered to herself.

Striding over to the bathroom phone, she dialed a number. "Hey, Daddy. Just wanted to hear your voice."

She smiled at the reply and, saying good-bye, hung up, satisfied. As she sank into the warm, soapy water, her body started to tingle with anticipation. Although she had hours to wait, she knew this wouldn't be like the dry, mechanical sex with Bullet. In all the years, eight to be exact, since she was eighteen, he had never failed to please her.

Mentally, she reviewed her schedule. The trunk of her car already had shopping bags from Nieman Marcus and Macy's in New Orleans stashed in it. She would have to run up to Edgewater Plaza to buy something for Bullet, and then swing by Mary Jane's to cement her alibi. Hopefully, when all this was done, it would be time to go see Sugar.

Chapter Three

Sugar's house, which he shared with Elnora, sat on a spit of land that jutted out into Biloxi's Back Bay. Located near the intersection of Creek and Hiller Roads, it had been built by a man who'd made millions in prostitution and gambling thirty years ago, when Biloxi had been the place to come for illicit needs along the coast.

At the top of the stairs, a long hall separated the west and east wings. Nora and Sugar both stayed on the west end of the house, in separate bedrooms. Four bedrooms, each with a small attached bath or shower, occupied the east end. Nora entered the largest of these rooms.

The little sitting room contained a small maple dinette with two place settings. She had done the bedroom and bath earlier, as well as prepared the other two rooms that would be used tonight. Placing the magnum of champagne in the ice bucket, she turned to leave.

For the thousandth time she wondered why she helped Sugar do this. Over the years, as his little game started and progressed, she saw that he needed help with the details. He was a fanatic about the little things.

So she gradually took on more and more of the setup. Now, all she had to know was whose night it was, and she took care of everything.

Her life had become one of very narrow focus. Sugar, what he wanted, and what he needed; this was her existence. Beyond that, she wouldn't, couldn't see. He'd tried to get her to open up, to even see a shrink, but she refused. What had happened to her had almost broken her completely.

She was content to withdraw from everyone and everything in the world. Except Sugar. Deep inside, she felt that helping him with his game kept her safer. As much as she downplayed and tried to hide her looks, sometimes he would look at her strangely. It made her stomach flutter. She would do anything for him, but the thought of THAT—of being touched like THAT—terrified her.

Sugar sat in the armchair located in the first bedroom off the stairs. A dresser, nightstand, and large bed were the only other furnishings. He was fully dressed, having showered after work. Although he had three different women to see within the next three hours, he wasn't concerned.

He didn't have to screw Mary tonight, the way he figured it. Neesha, well, that would be intense, but quick, and he smiled at the thought. Jessica, though, would take up the bulk of his time. One of his biggest secrets was that it wasn't just the sex that got him paid. Another was that all the girls in his game, as well as himself, had a long history together.

There was a gentle knock, and the door opened. He could just glimpse Nora in the hall as Mary entered, smiling.

"Hi, Sugar."

"Hey, baby." He rose and embraced her.

Mary had on a short, tight skirt. Her matching blouse did little to hide her huge breasts. She wore her hair short, framing a wide-cheeked, pretty face. She was five-six and full-bodied. She was by no means fat, but a few more years would take her there if she wasn't careful. Life as a pampered housewife had made her lazy.

Uh-oh, Sugar thought. The glaze in her eyes and the way her hands softly rubbed his back told him she had dropped a tab of X earlier. This could be a complication.

Mary was bored out of her skull with her routine, humdrum life. Sugar had sex with her less than with any of his girls. Mainly, she wanted to talk. Overall, she was satisfied with her husband and two kids, but there was something missing. Sugar, with their history together, and his particular brand of empathy provided what she needed.

"Are you okay, baby?" he asked, still embracing her.

"Yeah. No. I don't know. I'm kinda restless. I took a pill and had a drink. Me and Jess are supposed to be in New Orleans. I needed to see you."

Sugar broke the embrace, took her hand, and led her to the bed. He sat on the edge and coaxed her into his lap.

"Tell me."

Laying her head on his shoulder, she started to talk. As she recounted her day, starting with an argument with her husband and progressing through a day full of trials with her preschoolers, Sugar stroked her and listened quietly.

Mary's body was on fire. The ecstasy, the liquor, Sugar's touch, and the relief at getting her problems vented all seemed to make her juices flow. She started to wiggle in Sugar's lap, signaling her arousal.

"I'm sorry, baby. You told me earlier we only had a little time and you wanted to talk, but I need you." The plea in her voice was obvious.

Sugar didn't say anything. He undid her blouse and pulled it open. Undoing the clasp in the front of her bra, he allowed her tits to spring free. Lowering his head, he kissed her deeply, running his tongue into her mouth. She moaned into his mouth.

His hands found her nipples, big and hard between his fingers. Her movements had hiked her skirt up above her hips, and he could feel the heat of her pussy through his pants.

He spoke for the first time. "Stand up."

As he worked his slacks down over his erection, Mary ripped her skirt and wet panties off. She licked her lips at the size and length of his dick, undecided as to whether she wanted to feel it or taste it. He settled the question when he pulled her to him.

Mary climbed onto the bed, her knees straddling his hips. Sugar reached between her thighs with both hands. Spreading them wider, he cupped her ass and quickly lifted her onto him.

"Aaaah," Mary moaned as he slid deeply into her.

Sugar clung tightly to her ass, pulling her close so that they remained groin to groin, him throbbing inside her.

"Oh, shit," Mary moaned as an orgasm shook her, coming seemingly from nowhere.

Aware of the effects of the Ecstasy, Sugar rolled her over and began to fuck her. He stroked in and out with smooth, steady movements. Her pussy felt like hot velvet, and despite himself, he became caught up in the experience.

Mary lost track of how many times she came, the whole thing seeming like one continuous orgasm. She was vaguely aware of Sugar approaching his climax. His dick got harder and seemed to go deeper into her. Finally, with a groan, he buried himself inside her one last time. He was so far inside her, it bordered on pain. As his seed spurted into her, Mary had one last toe-curling orgasm, her juices bathing his length.

They lay gasping, tightly clutching each other.

"Good thing we didn't both drop some *X*," Mary said. "You might have killed me."

She kissed his face then held his head to her breasts. "Thanks, Sugar. You always do me right."

He got up and drew her along behind him to the bathroom. After they'd showered, Mary retrieved her bag from where she'd dropped it near the door. Extracting an envelope, she placed it on the dresser and got dressed.

Sugar, back in his chair, spoke before she opened the door. "Promise me something."

"What?"

"That you won't do any more Ecstasy until next week. It's our quality time, and I do want to talk to you. Okay?"

She hesitated a second, then turned and walked over to him. Kissing him on the cheek, she said, "Anything for you, baby." Then she left him.

As Mary drove home to her husband, John, and their kids, she practiced her usual procedure after playing Sugar's Game. Beating herself up. The short but intense sexual episodes, combined with Sugar's calming effect on her, had taken away the edge from her high.

The problem was, as she saw it, that she loved her husband and family. As a former prostitute, it wasn't the sex that she was guilt-tripping about. Even though John neither knew or suspected that she was fucking Sugar on a regular basis, it was still adultery.

John knew all about her past hooking. As a matter of

fact, he had gone from a regular trick (and unsuspecting participant in The Game), to a good husband, father, and provider.

What he didn't know was the hell in which she and her friends had grown up in. He knew about The Strip in general. John was from Jackson, though, and had never frequented the place.

There was no way for him to know that she felt that she owed her very survival to her group of friends: Sugar, Cole, Jessica, Alana, and Taneesha. The Strip chewed up its residents and spat them out. Very few of its young people reached adulthood without being irrevocably fucked up.

Mary and her friends had survived by sticking together. The bond between them was deep and permanent. The Game had started at a time in their lives when it was a matter of survival.

Now it was a habit. More than that, it was a way of keeping their bond fresh and alive, even though their lives had diverged. So they all felt obligated to continue playing.

Being honest, she had to admit to herself that the sex played a big part. Sugar could fuck! That nigga set her off like a pack of firecrackers. The very thought of what he'd done to her lifted her black mood.

"Yeah, you might be doing some fucked-up shit, but you doin' it with the right one," she said to herself.

Sighing, Mary fired up some weed, determined to go home and do to John what Sugar had just done to her.

CHAPTER FOUR

Sugar still sat in the chair, dressed in his robe, ten minutes later when Nora walked in. He was deep in thought, staring off into space, so he didn't notice the sad, wistful look that crossed her face as she looked at him. He started when she spoke.

"Taneesha will be here in about an hour."

"I'll be ready." He stood and walked out of the room.

After she stripped the bed, Nora took the envelope from the dresser. Opening it, she counted the money. *Twelve hundred dollars. Mary's husband must be doing really good.* She sighed, put the envelope in her pocket, and left.

An hour later, when Nora ushered Taneesha into her usual room, she noted that, as always, it was dark, except for one small-wattage lamp on the nightstand. Sugar lay on the bed naked. Nora couldn't help a quick peek. Her eyes took in his muscled thighs, flat stomach, and broad shoulders. What drew her attention, though, was the mast of his dick, stiffly waving between his legs. The sudden tightness in her stomach made her gasp as she averted her eyes and hurriedly closed the door.

At first glance, Taneesha looked like a typical White California beach bunny. High breasts, tight ass, and golden skin topped by a head of long, blond hair. However, she wasn't from California, she hated the beach, and she wasn't even White. So she definitely wasn't typical.

Without even greeting Sugar, she started to undress. When her clothes lay in a pile around her feet, she spoke. "I'm ready. Hump will kick my ass as it is. If I'm late for my next job, he'll really whip me."

"Well, he better make damn sure you like it 'cause, if you don't, I'll kick his ass all the way back to Slidell. Come here."

When she got close to the side of the bed, Sugar sprang up and grabbed a handful of her hair with his left hand. His right took one of her breasts and squeezed it hard. She moaned. Sugar threw her face-down on the bed and climbed up behind her.

Placing his palm down in the middle of her back, he held her in place. Withdrawing a leather paddle from beneath the pillow, he began to rhythmically spank her. At first the only sounds in the room were the *thwack* of the leather on her ass, and the soft grunts she made.

"Uh, unh, unh, unh, unh."

Each time he struck her, she grunted and her ass cheeks flexed, even as they reddened.

"Oh, baby, that's it. Harder, please, harder."

She rolled her ass side to side, trying to grind her throbbing pussy into the mattress. Sugar hit her harder. She began to twist. He could barely hold her with one hand.

"Yes. I'm ready now. Do it!"

Sugar threw the paddle to one side. Taking her by the waist he raised her to her knees. Positioning himself, he slid into her dripping pussy. She slammed her ass back against him, seeking a new kind of pain.

For a moment, he felt the heat of her reddened ass against his entire middle. Knowing what she wanted, he grasped her waist and began to pound into her as hard as he could. She met him stroke for stroke, her hair flying wildly as she tossed her head and screamed.

"Tear it up, baby. Hurt that pussy. Oh, oooh."

Sugar was so caught up in the act now, he feared her gyrations would separate them. He leaned his weight against her, forcing her to lie flat on the bed. Opening his legs, he trapped her thighs between his.

Now, she could only move a few inches up and down, and he was in control. He fucked her now with slow, even strokes. Forcing his hand beneath her, he squeezed her right nipple very hard.

She bucked and came. He could feel her pussy contract around him. Rising slightly, he pumped into her forcefully. His balls tightened as he spent himself inside her.

He rolled off her and they lay side by side. Sugar stared at the ceiling, feeling slightly guilty. What was wrong with him? As he spanked her, his arousal grew. While she writhed in pain, he was consumed with the desire to fuck her as brutally as he could. And he liked it.

Taneesha sensed his mood. He was usually like this after a session with her.

"Hey. Don't be like that. You know that's how I like it. It's the only way I can really get off. We both know why. You're the only one who can do me just right. Just enough hurt to make it feel real good. Not too much. And you got enough dick to make my pussy holler. Hump and all my customers are just money. I know I'm messed up. Don't you turn away too."

Sugar rolled over and took her in his arms. She relaxed against him, and they held each other.

"Sorry, Neesha. You know I'm always here for you. Next time we'll use the ropes."

He felt her body shiver in anticipation. Another twinge of sadness for her situation ran through him. Fuck it. She was his friend, and this was just how she was.

"Tell you what. You keep giving the customers straight sex or whatever, and I'll take care of all your special needs. Hump knows me, so tell him I said if he touches you like that—if I see one mark I didn't make—I'll kill him."

Now she was happy. Though he couldn't see her face, he could tell. That was all the reassurance she needed.

"Shit!" She jumped up and ran to the bathroom. "I'm late," she spoke over her shoulder. "Get my stuff together, and get the envelope out of my purse."

Ten minutes later, she was rushing out. When Nora came in, Sugar walked past her without looking at her.

"I'll be in Jessica's room," he mumbled.

Why, he's ashamed, Nora thought. *Good!* She hummed to herself as she cleaned up his mess.

CHAPTER FIVE

Taneesha sped away from Sugar's house. The hotel on the strip where she had her next "date" was only a leisurely fifteen-minute drive from where she was, but she was already five minutes late.

Hump was gonna be pissed. She quickly dialed the club on her cell phone.

"Hey, it's me. I'm running a little late . . ."

She listened to a minute of his usual tirade.

"Stop yelling at me! I just left Sugar's house. He gave me a message for you. And one from Cole."

That brought instant silence. Hump was connected with some pretty bad people, but he had been around The Strip a long time. He had survived by never fucking over his bosses and by knowing who was who on The Strip.

Fucking with Sugar wasn't a wise move, but fucking with Cole was straight suicide. Her lie about Cole's inadvertent message had the desired effect. Hump stopped bitching and said he'd call the trick and explain.

She sat back with a sigh and drove on. For a few minutes she could relax and enjoy the aftermath of the world-class fucking Sugar had just put on her. Personally, she hoped The Game never ended.

Taneesha knew that Sugar's participation in the rough sex that she got off on was reluctant. She hated to see the sadness in his eyes as he did the things he knew she needed to really get off.

She also guessed that he felt some guilt at the pleasure he got from physically abusing her. It was really fucked up that her pleasure was so dependant on pain, and Taneesha knew it. Several times she'd tried to enjoy "normal" sex, but it didn't work for her.

Fucking Armond.

Her mother was a whore just like all her friends' mothers were. Bonita was one of those prostitutes who considered herself "married" to her pimp. They had a little three-bedroom house a couple of blocks off The Strip.

Taneesha's father had been some anonymous White trick. She had been only eight years old when her mom took up with Armond. With the wisdom typical of street kids, Taneesha had been aware that it was her White-girl looks that kept him around just as much as the money he made from Bonita selling her ass.

When Taneesha turned twelve, her body started to really sprout. Armond started to pay her more and more attention. The way he looked at her and the way he always seemed to be hanging around when she bathed or got ready for bed started to worry her.

Growing up in the middle of Whorehouse Row, Taneesha had no illusions about what he wanted. She also had no illusions about what would happen if she told Bonita about her fears. Her mom was really sprung on Armond and worshiped his worthless ass.

Telling would only get her beat, or put out, or both. So she lived in fear and tried to avoid him. For a while it worked. Then the inevitable happened. One night, shortly after her thirteenth birthday, Armond made his move.

Bonita was out turning tricks, and Taneesha, sure that she was alone in the house, had taken a bath. She was drying off when the door flew open. Armond stood there, dressed in only a pair of shorts.

"Damn, Neesh. You packing, girl. Them little boys puttin' that meat in yo' life?"

"Get out of here, Armond! I'm-a tell Mama! I don't fuck with them no-good niggas, an' you ain't got no business in here."

"Listen, you little bitch! Get this straight—I run shit around here. You tell Bonita anything, I'm-a say you a lyin' little ho. Who you think she gonna believe? Now I'm gonna teach you how to be a woman. Them little-dicked boys can't do that. Come here."

Taneesha froze like a deer caught in headlights. Armond grabbed his belt from the hook behind the bathroom door and dragged her naked, clinging to her towel and hollering for her life, into his bedroom.

The next two hours were a nightmare. He didn't fuck her that night, but the torture began. Wielding the belt and overpowering her with his infinitely greater strength, he whipped her. Her legs, front and back, her ass, her back. The broad belt cut into her naked skin with sharp pain. After a while she couldn't fight anymore. When she surrendered, he stopped beating her.

Throwing her onto the bed, he climbed in with her. Putting both her legs over his shoulders, Armond reached up and grabbed both her young breasts roughly. Squeezing them painfully hard, he next did a thing that completely shocked her.

He bent and licked her pussy. When his rough tongue slid across her clit, the pain and pleasure overwhelmed her. She came for the first time with a shout. Her thighs locked around her stepfather's head as he continued to torture her quivering pussy.

Later he made her suck him off while he alternated slapping her ass cheeks hard and running his big finger over her love button. She came so hard that she hardly noticed his come sliding down her throat.

Taneesha lay awake the entire night. Her emotions see-sawed back and forth between anger, hatred, and shame. She hated Armond for what he'd done. She was deeply ashamed because, in spite of the pain and the fact that it was rape, she enjoyed it so much.

Over the course of the next three weeks, Armond repeated his act with her six times, each time waiting until Bonita was gone. By the fourth time, Taneesha could feel her pussy get wet when he reached for the belt.

The sixth time he took her cherry while beating her with a curtain rod. Taneesha lost count of the number of times she came. Armond was a pimp and he knew what he was doing. He could give a fuck that Taneesha was his stepdaughter. Now she was his sex slave too.

This went on for two years. By the time she was fifteen, Taneesha's mind was fucked-up. She equated physical pain with sexual fulfillment. Her mind was constantly filled with self-loathing and shame.

Armond was ready to start pimping her out to tricks who were into that type of thing. Her lush body and beauty would make him a fortune. Bonita would just have to fall in line. That's what hoes did.

Taneesha didn't tell anyone about Armond. Not even her friends. But then the attraction between her and Cole had become greater. His tough attitude and naturally surly disposition were irresistible to her.

The truth came out the first time they fucked. His shocked look when she begged him to hurt her drove her to tears. She felt like a freak. Cole wouldn't leave her alone. He held her in the whore's crib they had borrowed until she told him all of it.

His eyes burned with rage as he drove himself into her from behind, slapping her ass with each stoke. She came like never before. Cole told her not to worry.

Two days later Armond disappeared. A week after that, his body washed up on the jetty in Long Beach, ten miles away. Cole never said so, but Taneesha knew what he'd done. When things got hot for him, he left and ran to Houston. God, how she missed him.

She shook off her memories and went to work.

CHAPTER SIX

Sugar lay relaxing in the big bathtub. He was on his second glass of cognac, and he'd had to reheat the water once already. He didn't hear her come in, but he felt her presence. Opening his eyes, he saw her standing in the doorway.

"Hi."

"Oh, baby, I'm sorry I'm late. I had to shop, for real, and I spent more time at M.J.'s than I intended."

Sugar wondered how much of their earlier interlude Mary Jane had shared with her friend.

"It's okay, Jess. Chill. We can talk while we bathe. Come on."

He watched as she undressed, struck as always by the utter beauty and perfection of her body.

"Ow! You got it too hot as usual."

Reaching up, he chucked her behind both knees so that she collapsed into the water on top of him. Ignoring her short scream and the big splash, he turned so they sat facing each other, her legs across his thighs.

"Stop being such a baby. The hot water will relax you."

She extended her hand and squeezed his dick. "I don't need relaxing. I need this."

He smiled. "Later, greedy. We've got to bathe, eat, and talk. Then we'll worry about dessert."

For twenty minutes they washed and played, behaving like the carefree kids they had both once been. The constant touching caused sexual arousal in them both, but for Jessica, the undivided personal attention was just as important.

Later, they dried off and sat at the dinette, lazily picking at the seafood dinner left by Elnora. They talked of being raised in the little cottages behind the huge whorehouse off Southern Avenue where Jessica's mother worked and Sugar's Aunt Berea was the madam.

Sugar remembered Reuben, the big Samoan bouncer whose main job seemed to be keeping him out of trouble. Reuben's preferred method of discipline consisted of putting the young Sugar in boxing gloves and beating him silly. Later, starting when Sugar was thirteen, he took the gloves off and taught Sugar to really fight—to use his elbows, knees, and teeth and to show no mercy. He also taught him to shoot.

As a teenager, Sugar was the most feared boy on the block. Except for Cole. Any insult or slight to Mary Jane, Jessica, Taneesha, Alana, or their prostitute mothers brought on a fight, no matter how big or how old the opponent.

Jessica tearfully recalled being raped by one of her mother's drunken tricks at fourteen. How Reuben killed the guy. Sugar was in reform school and Cole on the run when it happened. Jessica and Taneesha got sent to a house across the bay and turned out.

The two girls had just returned to the house on Southern to work when Sugar got out. Boy, was he pissed to see his old friends turning tricks. Not for long, though.

It was an election year, and for one of the few times in its history, Biloxi got an honest mayor. Buford Johnson shut down the whorehouses and gambling parlors along the railroad.

Determined to not let his friends walk the streets, Sugar rented an old warehouse along the docks. He moved Jessica, Mary, Alana, and Taneesha in, and then went to work.

He shucked oysters, worked a shrimp boat, and did a host of other jobs so the girls could finish school. They spent many nights fending off hunger by sharing their dreams. Mary wanted to be a wife and mother, Taneesha a dancer, Alana a movie star, and Jessica just wanted to be rich.

All the girls loved Sugar. Sometimes they would argue as to who got to sleep with him, and they all did at times. He made them feel special. He was a true friend. Although he worked his ass off, they had nothing. So what happened next really wasn't so strange.

Sugar came stumbling in one night with this girl in tow. She was a mess. A big cut over one breast made it look like somebody tried to slice her tit off. Her thighs were bloody. There were big bruises all over her body, and her eyes were swollen shut.

Still, she was in better shape than Sugar. He'd been shot. The bullet had torn a big chunk of meat out of his side, and he'd obviously lost blood. Taneesha knew a nurse from the clinic and prevailed upon her to help. Sugar wouldn't let them call the cops or an ambulance.

The girl's name was Elnora. She was about their age, seventeen or eighteen, and she didn't speak more than two words for months. Something bad had gone down, and Sugar had saved her. After she got cleaned up, she wouldn't leave his side.

It was Jessica who started The Game. She was leaving

the employment office one day. Sugar hadn't been able to work, and they were getting desperate. A car pulled up alongside her. It was a local dealer named Joe. As he continually spit his game at her, she finally told him she had to find work. Her brother was sick and she didn't have time to mess around.

He made her an offer. Spend some time with him, and he'd take care of her bills. She gave him an address and a time to pick her up, and he gave her five hundred dollars. She went home, put Elnora out of Sugar's room, and crawled in bed with him. After they made love, she took the envelope with the money and laid it on the bed. Then she left to bathe and dress.

When he figured out what it meant, Sugar was pissed and started an argument with Jessica. Taneesha jumped his shit and then the others joined in. He needed them now, and he'd just have to live with it.

Alana was next to play the game. Soon it became a game amongst the girls to see who could hustle some guy, screw Sugar, and leave the most money.

That was how Sugar's Game got started. It enabled him to buy things for them, even to start his restaurant. Now, even though he didn't really need the money and they all had lives, they still did it. Maybe it kept something of their youth alive. Or maybe it was a protest against the lives they'd been pushed into.

"Fuck it," Jessica said. "I don't care how we got here, I know what I want." She got up from the table and led him to the bedroom.

CHAPTER SEVEN

Sugar watched Jessica's fine, round ass twitch as he followed her into the bedroom. He wanted her. Of course, any straight male between the ages of ten and ninety would desire her. She was just that fine. He also cared about her. Deeply. It wasn't love, though.

Sugar was pretty sure that she knew. And that it hurt her. Because of that, out of all his special girls, he took the most time and care with Jessica. As if to make up for the way he didn't feel. She stopped at the edge of the bed and he came up behind and wrapped his arms around her.

The touch of her ass against his dick made it twitch, and the caress of his palms made her nipples harden instantly. Brushing her hair aside with his nose, he nibbled at the back of her neck while his hands roamed her breasts. She let out a deep sigh and pushed her butt into his crotch.

His right hand wandered lower, across her stomach, to the top of her mound. Cupping her, he let the index finger separate the lips of her pussy. Her juices immediately coated it. When the tip of his finger touched the little bud at the top, she squirmed and let her legs relax, opening herself up to his hand.

Sugar turned her around. After sucking his finger, he bent to kiss her, letting her taste herself. Jessica's hands roamed his back, grabbing at his ass as the kiss deepened. She was fully aroused, her pussy dripping. Ready for him.

Without breaking the kiss, Sugar lay her down on the bed. Kneeling to one side of her, he again fingered her pussy, letting his finger slide into its moist depth. Jessica moaned into his mouth. She pulled frantically at his fully erect dick. Sugar wasn't about to be rushed, though.

Breaking the kiss, he let his tongue trail down her neck and between her breasts.

Turning his head to one side, he licked up the side of one breast, then sucked the nipple into his mouth, biting gently on in.

Her crotch bucked against his hand. "Oooh, yes," she moaned.

After doing the other nipple, his tongue continued its journey south. Toying with her navel momentarily, he halted when he reached her bush. Withdrawing his hand, he ignored her soft protest. Slowly and deliberately, he raised her hips and placed two pillows under her.

With her ass raised and her head and shoulders flat on the bed, the lower part of her body was easier to access. Sugar spread her legs and knelt between them. Without prelude, he lowered his head and licked the length of her pussy.

"Shit, baby. That feels so good," she panted.

Suppressing a smile, Sugar placed one hand on each

thigh and, using his thumbs, opened her folds. Then he went to work on her. He licked her, sucked her, then ran his tongue in and out of her. When he took her clit gently between his teeth, she lost it. His strong hands held her pinned while his tongue continued to assault her throughout her orgasm.

He only relented when she went limp. She lay, glistening in sweat, panting, her beautiful face still distorted by pleasure. As she caught her breath, she hardly noticed him systematically rubbing the liquid from her pussy all over the head of his dick. He moved forward on his knees.

In almost one motion he raised her legs, threw them over his shoulders, and pushed forward into her. He grabbed her ass and pulled her down onto his dick.

"Aaah! Aaah," she shouted, more in surprise than anything.

With her ass in the air, he slid all the way in, their groins locked together. He held her there, buried inside her, gripping her ass tightly.

After a minute, she began to strain upward against him, and he could feel her pussy relaxing and re-lubricating around him. It was time.

Slowly he eased himself out of her, until only the head remained. Sliding back in halfway, he repeated the motion. In and out. In and out. Soon she was snapping her hips upward, trying to take more. She felt so good around him, and her frantic desire excited him even more.

Despite his intentions to slow-fuck and eat her into a coma, he felt his detachment fading. Placing his palms flat on the bed, he began to work his hips, plunging deeply into her with each stroke. She smiled, knowing that she had him now.

Soon the only sounds to be heard were skin on skin, along with Sugar's soft grunts. Jessica peaked first again.

Her hot pussy gripping at him sent him over. He grabbed her ass again as he pumped his seed into her. He spurted over and over until he was drained.

Totally sated, he collapsed on top of her, careful to take most of his weight on his elbows. He waited for his breathing to slow enough for him to talk.

"Damn, girl. That pussy of yours ought to be against the law."

She giggled. "It used to be. Remember?"

He rolled off her, his dick leaving her with a wet *plop*. Sitting up, he looked at her. "I've got to shower and crash. We open early, you know. You heard from Cole lately? He didn't call me last week."

Jessica reluctantly got up and headed toward the bathroom. Speaking over her shoulder she said, "Far as I know, Cole is still hustling in Fifth Ward. I wish he'd come home. I've got to go first. I need to get home."

Their childhood friend John Coleman, whom they called "Cole," had recently been released from a Texas prison. As a kid, Sugar was a fighter, but Cole had always been a killer. He'd had to leave Biloxi as a teenager after killing a man. He'd run to Houston. A few years later, he caught five for manslaughter.

Sugar had kept his books fat while he was in the Darrington State Pen, but Cole didn't return to Biloxi when he got out. He called almost every week and promised to come home when he finished his "business" in Texas.

Jessica, dressed now, came over to the bed. Dropping an envelope on to it, she took Sugar's face in her hands.

"Oh, Sugar."

Her heartbeat doubled, but she bit back what she was about to say and kissed his cheek.

"Bye."

"Be careful, baby."

After she left, he picked up the envelope. No need to count it; he knew there would be several thousand dollars in it. On average, he netted around two hundred thousand a year from his little game. He told himself again that it wasn't about the money.

CHAPTER EIGHT

As she drove away from Sugar's house, Jessica realized that she had just dodged a bullet. A big, fat, deadly emotional bullet. She had come real close to pouring her heart out to Sugar and telling him exactly how she felt. And this was something she had sworn never to do.

She supposed that it was only natural that she feel this proprietary attitude toward him, since she knew him first. Hell, they started pre-school together. Adria, Jessica's mother, had a little four-room house right next door to where Sugar lived with Tichi, Reuben's wife.

Tichi had cared for Sugar since he was a baby. In fact, that was who he got his name from. Tichi had called him Sugar when he was little and it just stuck.

Since Adria and Sugar's Aunt Berea spent their nights in the big whorehouse a hundred yards in front of the cottages, the two children were often together under Tichi's care. They were inseparable.

When they were six years old, they used to sneak into the big house through the kitchen. Hiding in closets or under the big four-poster beds, they saw and heard the whole gamut of the whorehouse experience.

A few months later Tichi caught them in Sugar's bedroom trying out the things they had seen the prostitutes do. An outraged Tichi spanked their little asses, but Adria and Berea just laughed.

Jessica had Sugar all to herself until second grade. Then Cole showed up. His mother worked for Berea too. Cole had lived until then with his grandmother in Ocean Springs, a little town just across the bay from Biloxi.

With no other family after his grandmother died, he was brought to live with Tichi, and shared a room with Sugar. After the usual male posturing, the two boys became fast friends. If it had been left up to Cole, Jessica would have been excluded from their boyish games, but Sugar wouldn't hear of it.

Over the course of the next year, Alana and Mary, both daughters of house prostitutes, joined their little set. Taneesha, although she lived a couple of streets away, spent all her free time with the group.

The six kids virtually had the run of the whole strip. They harassed and made fun of the tricks, stole toys and fruit from neighborhood stores, snuck off to the beach a few blocks away, and generally got into all the kinds of shit a group of unsupervised children could.

It wasn't all fun and games, though. They lived in a world of greed, sex, and violence. For them to bear witness to robbery, rape, violent assault, and occasionally murder, wasn't unusual.

Reuben's fearsome reputation kept them physically safe for a while. That and the fact that the house prostitutes as a group adopted them. Those whores had enough weapons between them to equip a small army. And a reputation for using them.

So Jessica, Sugar, and their friends were safe enough as

children on The Strip. But few things in nature can be as cruel as a mean-spirited child. At school they were outcasts. "Bastards from The Strip."

They all learned to play the dozens, all the while hiding the hurt because it wasn't really "playing" on their part. Their mothers, aunts, and friends really *were* whores. But in their world you didn't show weakness. That was suicide.

So they fought. It soon became known that if you took on one of the six—male or female—you had to fight them all. When Reuben took Sugar and Cole and taught them how to really fight, to maim and kill, things got easier.

Any insult to Sugar or his friends would set him off. He fought with a cold ferocity and intent that thrilled Jessica. He spent a lot of time in detention.

As dangerous as Sugar was in a fight, though, Cole was much worse. When Sugar's opponent broke weak and gave up, he backed off and let them slink or crawl away. Not Cole. Provoking him was sure to get your ass stomped into a mud hole—if you were lucky.

Once, Jessica and Taneesha were at their lockers in middle school. They were thirteen, and both girls' bodies were ripening into womanhood. Two big jocks from the football team got it into their heads to push up on them.

Because of what their mothers did for money, boys automatically assumed the girls were fucking. These niggas knew these two fine-ass girls hung with Sugar and Cole, but that day, they just said, "Fuck it."

When Jessica told them to step off, they got rough. The biggest one pushed her up against the locker and stuck his hand up her skirt, feeling her ass. His friend had Taneesha from behind, with both hands on her tits.

They were so inflamed by lust that neither noticed when the hallway got quiet and the students milling around and egging them on backed away. Jessica noticed. Even in the midst of her scratching and kicking attempts to get the boy's hands off her, she saw Cole appear behind them like a ghost.

Reuben had given them all knives. They were specially made folding weapons with five-inch blades. The heavy steel was honed to a razor sharpness. Without opening the blade or saying a word, Cole delivered a short, vicious blow to the back of the boy's head—the one assaulting Jessica.

Even as his groping hands released her and his slumping weight crushed her against the locker, Jessica saw Cole lock his arm across the boy's throat and apply pressure. With a roar of rage, Jessica's assailant rose and reached for Cole.

Sugar spun him around and started to pummel him. It was something to see, Sugar pounding this guy's face and body like a machine. Finally, with blood pouring from his broken nose, the boy collapsed in defeat.

"Aargh!"

Sugar turned at the sound. Choked almost to the point of unconsciousness, the big linebacker stood and swung his shoulders in a desperate attempt to shake himself free from the smaller Cole.

The *click* was loud in the silence as Cole opened his knife. Arms and feet moving at fantastic speed, he began to kick and slice the boy. Cries of pain and fear were ignored as blood flew. Cole never stabbed him. He seemed intent on slicing him to pieces.

Had Sugar not heard the security guards and cops forcing their way through the crowd, the boy would have been dead meat. Cole was in a zone. Sugar, Jessica, and Taneesha knew, but what the fuck? The niggas started it.

The fallout was serious. They dragged Sugar and Cole downtown and took the football players to the hospital.

The principal had told the cops that Sugar and Cole, along with those "fast" girls they hung out with, were a bunch of young troublemakers.

Reuben rushed Jessica and Taneesha to the police station. The guy in charge, a Detective Farelli, backed off when the girls said they were saved from an attempted rape and would press charges. Sugar and Cole were warned that one more incident would land them in reform school.

A little more than a year later Sugar was in the state boys' home and Cole was on the run for killing some guy in a nightclub. Life changed dramatically for Jessica and the girls.

Less than two weeks after Cole left, Jessica was in her bedroom with her headphones on, listening to a CD. Julius, one of her mother's regular tricks, decided to come looking for Adria, when he was told she wasn't working that night. She wasn't home either.

The drunken trick crashed in Jessica's door and mumbled something about "seeing if your pussy is as good as your ho-ass mama's." Jessica fought and screamed, but Julius was too strong.

The pain she felt between her legs as he forced himself into her was tremendous. He slammed into her over and over. Suddenly, the weight was gone. Reuben, having heard the screams from next door, had told Tichi to call the cops and rushed over.

Jessica actually heard the "snap" of Julius' neck breaking through her pain and tears. The cops called it justifiable homicide. Adria blamed Jessica.

Bonita, angry with Taneesha and blaming her for the death of Armond, convinced Adria that since both their daughters were "little hoes," they might as well get paid. The two girls were sent to Berea's sister's whorehouse across the bay for a couple of years.

They were turned out. With Sugar and Cole gone, their little clique was destroyed. Berea sent for them three months before Sugar got out. Even before the house closed, though, Sugar never looked down on them because of what they had become.

Alana and Mary were also in the business. While he never brought recriminations against any of them, Jessica knew that the life they lived was eating him up inside. Once again, though, they were together again. They were family. Sugar belonged to all of them, so Jessica held her peace.

Chapter Nine

Bullet drove away from the liquor store on Keller Avenue. He'd bought a "short dog" of Cisco. It was an odd irony that the wine he chose to make his "lean" had the same name as his biggest problem. Francisco De Leon was his connection.

He and Cisco had been doing business for years. On average, Bullet bought at least twenty birds from the Puerto Rican each month. Now he needed to up his average, and the smart-ass greaser didn't want to come down on the price. He'd have to talk to him about that tonight.

Sipping his drink, he took a right off Howard Avenue onto Nixon. Pulling in to the driveway of a run-down two-story house, he killed the Navigator's engine. He sat and watched the street for a minute.

There were no lights showing in the windows, but, once his eyes adjusted, he could see shadowy movement way back on the right side. That would be the customers walking over from Elmer or Main. No prospective buyer was allowed to come to the front door.

Turning his gaze upward, he saw a dark shadow on

the second-floor balcony. That would be Trey. Bullet paid the corrupt town to leave them alone, but that wouldn't stop some wannabe gangster or crazed dope fiend from trying to crash his party.

He got out of the SUV and walked up on the porch. The door opened before he reached it.

"Yo, Bullet. What's up, home?"

The whispered voice belonged to Ace, who ran the place for him.

"What's up, Ace?" He gave his boy some dap and moved deeper into the room.

There was no furniture on the first floor, except for in the kitchen. All the windows were painted black, and the interior lights couldn't be seen from outside. The front and rear doors were made of steel, and all the windows had bars.

As they walked through to the kitchen, Bullet asked, "How'd the new batch work out?"

"It weighed. The hoes are upstairs bagging it now. I got you ready too."

The long kitchen table was covered with little plastic bags. Some had single crack rocks in them, and others had multiple stones. The two men on the other side of the table threw up deuces, and the one in the corner with the shotgun nodded at Bullet. There was a tap on the steel door. One of the men slid open a panel.

"Hey. Let me get a wholesale fifty."

"Who dat?"

"Leon, man!"

"Gotcha."

A crumpled fifty-dollar bill in a grimy hand came through the panel.

Brew took it and held it up to the dim light. Wordlessly, he selected a bag from the table and pushed it through to the crackhead. As Bullet jerked his head toward the door, another tap came on the panel.

The two men walked through the front room to the stairs. Walking down the upstairs hallway to the rear, Bullet held out his hand to stop Ace. Soft sounds were coming from behind a closed door.

Both men pulled their pistols. When Bullet jerked the door open, it was all he could do not to laugh. A young woman was bent over at the waist in the small utility closet. Her skirt was hiked up, and a man was fucking her.

The man was so into what he was doing, it took a few seconds for Bullet and Ace's presence to register. As he pumped into the girl, her head bumped the wall. This was what Bullet had heard.

Ace tapped the guy in his temple with the barrel of his gun.

"What you doin', nigga?"

"Ace! I was, I was just . . ."

"Yeah, I see."

Bullet reached past Ace and jerked the girl into the hallway by the hair. He bent her head back and looked into her eyes. Her pupils were fine, which meant she hadn't been smoking. She was humping for a promise of future dope. He let go of her hair and slapped her. Hard.

As she fell against the wall, hand going to her face, Bullet growled, "Git back to work, bitch. I ought to kick your ho ass."

The girl ran off.

The guy stood there, wide-eyed, dick shriveled in fear.

"Conch, how long you work fo' me?"

"Ten months, Bullet."

"Pull yo' pants up, boy."

As he did and stepped from the closet, Bullet turned to Ace.

"Who's lookin' out on Elmer Street?"

"Junebug."

"Get him up here to help watch the bitches. I'm-a send Conch here to take his place."

Ace pulled his cell phone and walked off a couple of paces, and Conch started to relax. That's when Bullet hit him. He went upside his head two or three times with his gun and, when Conch fell, used his boots. When he stopped, the young man was a bloody, shivering mess.

"You pull some shit like this again, I'll bust a cap in yo' ass. Git yo' dick wet on your own time. Got me?"

Conch nodded his head.

"Go on down an' watch the back street. An' don't fuck up."

The boy crawled away.

"Sorry 'bout that. I was counting your package just before you came," Ace said.

"Ain't yo' fault. Nigga wanna fuck, I understand that, all that half-naked pussy standing around. But bizness is bizness. One nigga watchin', hoes could steal me blind."

They continued on to the back room. The wall had been knocked down, making one huge room. Along one of the remaining walls sat a row of Bunsen burners, each attached to a small propane tank. None were lit now, as Bullet's cooker had rocked up five kilos of cocaine earlier.

Most of the remainder of the room was taken up by three long tables. The first was manned by three women, one of whose face was still swelling from Bullet's blow. The three were systematically breaking down the dope. One scored the long, nine-inch-wide slabs with an Exacto knife. The girl in the middle broke the slabs into thin strips with her gloved hands. The end woman cut the strips into twenty-dollar rocks and placed them in a bin.

The table in the middle had two positions. At the first, a girl weighed the rocks and trimmed the excess. The shavings went into a bowl beside her. Her companion bagged the stones into one-, five-, and ten-stone packs.

The lone man at the third table took the bags, counted them, wrote down the tally, and placed them in a gym bag. A youth with an AK-47 leaned against one wall. Bullet walked up to him.

"Yo, man. What's up wit' Conch?"

"Say, Bullet. Ho say she gotta go piss, C-man say he take her. I don' know nothing else."

Bullet knew he was lying, but could appreciate the way he stood up for his partner. He decided to let it go. The girls were all crack hoes, anyway. They worked nearly naked and were paid daily in dope and money, even if there was no product to work. Those days they could sell all the blowjobs and pussy to his men they wanted to.

The rule was, though, no fucking around when there was dope to be worked. Heaven help the bitch who tried to steal from him or set it up. It had only happened once, and that ho's titties sat on a table in the corner in a jar of formaldehyde. It was an effective reminder.

Turning on his heels, Bullet led Ace from the room and back down the hall. Ace stopped and opened a metal door with multiple locks. The table in this room contained a large gym bag. Inside was $200,000 cash. This was the money from the last five birds cooked. For Bullet, it was a week's gross.

Thirty minutes later, Bullet was taking an on-ramp onto the 110 Bridge across the Back Bay. A carload of his boys rode in front of him, and two more in back. They would escort him home. He decided to wait until tomorrow to talk to Cisco.

As he drove, he thought of the women that worked in his rock house. They were nothing like Jessica. He had one of the most beautiful women on the coast, and she was easy to live with. When he took her from Joe, he knew she'd be expensive. She spent a lot, but he had it to give, and she was worth it.

Good pussy, plus, she only hung out with Mary Jane, Alana, and that plain-ass Elnora. She didn't go to clubs a lot and he'd never seen her come on to another dude. He'd better not ever see it. He couldn't wait to wake her up and slip some dick to her.

CHAPTER TEN

Francisco De Leon stared vacantly at the floor-length windows in his condo, located in the deep curve where Bayview Street turned into Bayview Avenue. The east windows were painted a soft orange by the rising sun. The crystal chimes Alana had hung threw an explosion of rainbow colors across the ceiling.

His body jerked as Alana's warm mouth pulled at the crown of his dick. He lay spread-eagle on the bed, lost in the sensations his woman was creating. The cocaine he'd just snorted only intensified the experience.

Alana had woken minutes ago and started right in on him. Why, he didn't know and didn't care. She was worth every bit of the aggravation she sometimes caused him. Her lips and tongue worked their way back down his shaft to its base, where her hands gripped him tightly.

Her eyes looked up at him through the veil of her long, black hair, and she smiled. As always, he was struck by her beauty. As much as she hated to hear anyone say it, and everyone did, she looked like a big-breasted J-Lo. Ass for days, a 34D cup, and long, silky hair.

His dick jerked, as much from the thought of sliding past that huge ass into her silky pussy as from her present ministrations. As if reading his mind, she pulled her mouth off him with a soft *pop* and sat up. Squatting astride him, she placed his rod at her opening.

Slowly, slowly, she lowered herself onto him. Her face screwed into a moue of pleasure as she absorbed his meat. Thigh muscles flexing, she began to ride him. He reached around her and filled his hands with her big, soft ass. Squeezing rhythmically, and occasionally pulling the cheeks apart, he let her set the pace. She leaned forward slightly so that he could take first one, then the other nipple in his mouth.

The pace increased. Now she was slamming herself down on him, and he was rising to meet her. She made soft sounds, and as the volume increased, he could hear her.

"Papi, oh, Papi, yes."

She was close. He could feel the tremors starting deep inside her. He had been holding himself back, and now he let go of his rigid control. Thrusting upward as hard as he could, he began to come. As his hot seed flooded her, Alana screamed and her pussy clamped him like a vise.

They writhed in mutual ecstasy for a while, then lay still. Her lush breasts were crushed against his chiseled chest. His hands gently roamed her body as she languidly rotated her butt, milking the last drop of pleasure from their lovemaking.

As if their minds were as much in tune as their bodies, they started to speak at the same time.

"Alana."

"Papi."

"You first," she said.

He collected his thoughts. "I'm gonna keep it real with

you, Mama. You know me, and you know what I do. Up until about a year ago, even though we had already been together for a while, you was just my current thing. If one of them freaks out there turned me on, well, I just took care of my business."

He felt her whole body tense, and hesitated.

"Now don't get mad. I'm telling it like it is. I'm a man, and things were different then."

Reining in her hot Latin temper, Alana forced herself to be calm. *The Cabron!* Then the thought of her and Sugar crossed her mind, and guilt replaced the anger.

"Go on," she whispered.

Feeling her relax, he continued, "Then I had to go to San Juan, remember? All that fine Puerto Rican pussy all around, and I'm hangin' with the ballers, but all I could think of was you. I kept calling you all times of day an' night. I wan't checking on you, I was missing you."

Alana remembered how he kept calling. A couple of times she was with Sugar when he did. She also knew how much it was costing a man like Cisco to say this.

"That's when I started to know that you was beginning to mean more to me than the business. Then I knew it was time to get out. I've been lucky, but I also keep my mind on what I need to, stay ready to do whatever. Now, I just want something else."

Her head jerked, but he wasn't through yet.

"Mama, what I'm trying to say is, I want something more for us. I want a home an' children—lots of little *niños*. I want you to be my wife."

Alana lowered her head onto his chest, her mind whirling. This had to be a sign. She had been getting ready to leave him. Not because of Sugar, just the opposite. The more she thought about it, the more she realized how much she really cared for him. Until then, she'd not given a damn about any man but Sugar. She was going to leave because she'd always believed Sugar was the only man who cared about Alana, the woman.

The silence was pregnant. When Alana raised her head, her smile was wide.

"Papi! Oh, Cisco, I love you. I didn't know, I didn't think . . ."

The tears came. He wrapped his arms around her and breathed a sigh of joy and relief. Reaching for the bedside stand, he picked up what he'd put there earlier.

"Mama? I got something for you."

When Alana saw the size of the diamond ring he held, she squealed, "Oh! Oh! It's beautiful. Thank you!"

Placing the ring on her finger, she threw herself on him. Before either of them knew what was happening, she was on her knees, and he was pumping in and out of her. It seemed like they fucked for hours.

Afterward, while Francisco slept beside her, Alana reached another decision. Tonight would be the last time she played Sugar's Game. Just the thought made her fearful. She would be turning her back not just on Sugar, but on the girls too. They had all been the one constant in her life.

In between bouts of sex, she and Cisco had made plans. They were leaving. Not just Mississippi, but the country. They were rich, and both of them wanted to start over. She took her cell phone and went into the bathroom.

Francisco woke up when Alana got out of bed. The glow of satisfaction he felt came from a lot more than the great sex he and Alana had just had. He had just made what he considered the wisest and most beneficial decisions of his life.

Cisco had come up hard. The beautiful tropical paradise that most tourists considered Puerto Rico to be was only an illusion. For the natives, the vast majority of them anyway, it could be hell on earth.

The life expectancy of those born and raised in the island's vast, teeming slums was only a fraction of that in the more prosperous western countries. A mixture of Black slave ancestors, Latin colonists, and indigenous island Indians, the Ricans were just another "nigger minority" in the cities of its "host," the United States.

Like most starving, oppressed minorities, Puerto Rico's poor had to resort to criminal acts in order to have any chance at the good life. Given the choice of joining the expatriate Cubans, the military, or the drug lords, Cisco chose the latter.

He got his start at an early age running errands for his kinsman, Oscar Fuentes. He graduated to collecting debts. Never hesitant to use a gun or a knife, Cisco rose quickly up the ranks of Oscar's empire.

The collapse and rebuilding of the giant South American drug cartels and their smuggling route brought new business opportunities to Fuentes. He negotiated the entire Mississippi Gulf Coast as his territory, from Mobile, Alabama to Slidell, Louisiana. And he took Cisco with him.

In addition to huge fees for importing and warehousing vast amounts of cocaine, Fuentes received a percentage of all the sales in his area. Cisco and Jesse Verdun were key to this percentage as Oscar's distributors in Biloxi and Gulfport.

The years in Mississippi had been good to Francisco. He had more money than he could ever spend. So much, in fact, that he decided to leave the house, cars, and most of the possessions right there. Just walk away. Give them to Bullet.

He had already met with Fuentes a couple of days ago.

Normally, leaving an organization like this would be dangerous. The fact that Fuentes was a relative, coupled with the fact that Cisco had thought out all the logistics so that the money and dope kept flowing, had paved the way for him.

There was only one more piece of the plan he needed to implement before he made Bullet's day. Hell, his year! He picked up the phone and dialed.

"*Amigo*, it's me. You on a clean phone? Good. Uncle Oscar is gonna talk to you about this, but I wanted to tell you myself. I'm getting ready to bail. Real soon.

"You gon' be the man up here too. Nigga works for me is gonna move up. Name of Bullet. He's been doin' big things around here. I know you had that little mistake with him a while back, but that's old.

"You cool with that? Good. Uncle O will work out the details. I'm gonna meet with my boy later tonight and run it down to him. I'll have him call you on this phone. Yeah. I'm getting out an' gettin' hitched. Who else? Don't hate, *muchacho*. Later."

Cisco lay back and wondered if it was just his imagination or if Jesse was a little eager to work with Bullet. He'd let Alana deliver the message to Bullet. She was gonna have to see Jessica and her other girlfriends.

He lay back and let his mind fantasize about the new life he and Alana would have. His kids would never have to hustle or go hungry. Or pick up a gun. He drifted back to sleep imagining how it would be.

Chapter Eleven

John Joshua Coleman was impatient. He figured this was his most prominent and worst character trait. Everybody, and that included his friends, thought of him as a killer, and he was. Part of the reason for that was, he had no patience for bullshit. If you disrespected him or threatened him or somebody he cared about, then he'd as soon cap you as look at you.

His approach had seemed logical and sane to him, but he made a stab at conforming during his recent five-year bid in Texas Department of Corrections. He took anger management, and even paid attention in class. He even knew what a paradigm was. It was an interesting way to look at how to handle your problems, but his way was faster, more efficient, and permanent.

Still, he tried.

He slowly drove westward down Lyons Avenue. Shortly after crossing Gregg, he saw the man he was looking for posted up in front of a liquor store. He continued on, turning around in front of the funeral home.

Heading back up Lyons in the opposite direction, he worked to get his anger under control.

He was driving a new Cadillac, a gift from Jose for keeping it real when he got popped. Even though the cops tried to get him to talk, Cole kept his mouth shut about Jose and his criminal activity. Now, out of prison for about a month, he was waiting on one of Jose's runners to bring him some cash so he could split Houston. He wanted to go home.

He had left Biloxi on the run at age sixteen. Some nigga in The Blue Note, a club on Main Street, had gotten in his face about a girl who asked him to dance. Sugar was at the bar, or Cole probably would have just kicked the dude's ass. As it was, Cole stabbed him. With Sugar and Jessica's help, he ran to Houston's Fifth Ward.

After fucking up a couple of wannabes on Della Street, he was approached by a Mexican drug dealer named Jose from Denver Harbor. Jose needed somebody to guard his drug and money shipments to and from the Rio Grande Valley. Cole went to work for him.

A couple of years later, he was leaving his employer's house just off Wayside. This hot Mexican chick walked up and started a conversation just as he was getting into his Benz. One thing led to another, and soon he was knocking her down in a local motel.

The door burst open, and this Mexican dude charged in, screaming and cursing in Spanish. When he slapped the girl, Cole stepped in. The boy ended up dead. He ended up copping to manslaughter. Five years in hell.

Now he was doing a little slinging and a few collections until his money came through. He'd collect his ends and go see Sugar, and Jessica. Recently, from Sugar, he'd found out things weren't the way he thought they were between those two. If only he'd known ten years ago.

Pulling up in front of the liquor store, he parked and took his pistol from under his right thigh. The guys standing there tried to see into the car through the tinted windows. Cole opened his door and quickly stood, pointing his pistol across the car roof at the group.

"Nobody move! Brownie, get your ass over here."

Like smoke, everybody stepped away from a short, skinny, brown-skinned man, who stood wide-eyed and trembling, staring at Cole.

"C! Man, I was just looking for you. I got—"

"I said, git over here, nigga!"

Brownie, taking little baby steps, shuffled off the curb and around the front of the car. Cole grabbed him by the neck of his T-shirt and dragged him along the side of the 'Lac to the rear.

"Why you wanna fuck with me, man? I told you don't make me come looking fo' you. It's been a week and a half."

Letting go of Brownie's shirt, Cole popped the trunk. He cut in on Brownie's stammered excuses.

"Get in, nigga."

"Wh-what?"

Cole rapped him on the top of the head with the butt of the automatic. "Get in the trunk. Now."

Brownie half fell into the trunk's well. He barely tucked his legs in before Cole slammed the lid shut and drove off, headed back up Lyons. Feeble thumps sounded from the rear.

"I told you I wasn't nobody to fuck with!"

BAM!

Still driving, Cole had reached behind him and shot into the back seat of the car. There was a muffled scream.

"Jive-ass punk!"

BAM!

"Dope-fiend trick!"

BAM!

He turned left on Gregg, and by the time he'd crossed Liberty Road and pulled up in front of the abandoned apartments near the freeway, he'd blasted off three more shots. Slamming the gearshift into PARK, he got out and opened the trunk. None of the shots had hit Brownie, but he hadn't intended them to. Nor did he intend what he *did* find.

"Damn, punk, you done shit yourself."

Indeed, the quivering Brownie had dumped a load. The smell was horrendous. Cole had literally scared the shit out of him.

"Please, don't kill me, Cole. I'm sorry. I got most of yo' money in my pocket. Please."

The dude was actually crying.

"It ain't about the funky two hundred. It's about respect. You didn't show me none. Good thing I'm in a good mood. Get out of my ride, an' don't leave none of that shit in there."

Brownie carefully rolled out of the trunk onto the asphalt. He dug into his pocket and handed up a wad of bills.

"Ain't but ten dollars short. I swear."

Cole almost felt sorry for the dude. Almost.

"Get the fuck outta here. You ain't ridin' with me smelling like that."

Brownie stumbled off toward the row houses on Gregg. Cole got into his car and sat awhile. *Looks like that anger management shit did some good,* he thought. *I didn't kill the little motherfucker. Man, I need to get outta here.*

He drove off thinking of the beautiful Biloxi sunsets.

Chapter Twelve

One thought let to another. Ten years was a long time, and Cole had seen and done a lot of shit since he'd left home. After his grandmother's death, he had no blood relatives that he gave a fuck about.

His family was Sugar, Jessica, Taneesha, Alana, and Mary. They were the people who made him homesick for the Coast. The drama and hardships they'd all suffered through had welded a bond between them that was much deeper than mere friendship.

Leaving Biloxi and staying gone so long was hard. But it wasn't like he had much choice. That asshole in The Blue Note wasn't the first man he'd killed, or last. His mind strayed back to his first murder.

Armond never saw it coming. When Taneesha told Cole what was going on, a rage like he'd never known filled him. His first thought was to go get his boy Sugar and confront the bitch-ass, sadistic, child-raping mother-fucker.

He stopped himself, not wanting to get Sugar caught

up in what his heart knew was going to be a killing. The plan just came to him whole. Two days after Taneesha had confessed her situation, Cole made his move. It was on a Friday.

Catching Taneesha in the school hallway before sixth period, he told her to round up Jessica and the girls and meet him at Sugar's house. He stressed that she not go home first and to wait until he came to Sugar's. He told Sugar he would be there by seven o'clock.

As soon as the bell for last period rang, Cole slipped away from school. He went straight to Taneesha's house and knocked on the door.

"Hey, Mr. Armond, can I talk to you for a minute?"

Armond looked at him curiously. "Cole! What up, little nigga? Something wrong?"

"Yes, sir. It's Taneesha. She's pretty fucked-up. I don't know what she's gonna do. I figured I better come get you."

"What the fuck are you talkin' about? Where is she? I'm-a kill that little bitch!"

"She's on the old Bay Bridge. Talkin' about being pregnant, an' you, an' killing herself. I told her I was gonna go get Jessica an' Mary an' would be right back."

Armond's eyes went wide. Cole had played his role so well that Armond went along with it.

"C'mon, boy. You better show me where she is."

The old Bay Bridge was an incomplete concrete causeway that jutted about a mile out into the bay between Biloxi and Ocean Springs. It never occurred to Armond to wonder how Cole had traveled the three or four miles from the bridge to his house. He opened the passenger door to his Lincoln and let Cole in. They hauled ass for the bridge.

The old causeway was closed to automobile traffic. Those wanting to fish or just to enjoy the open water had to walk out onto the concrete roadway. A wooden gate stretched completely across the end of the bridge about thirty feet from the point where it abruptly terminated.

Armond followed Cole's fast-paced walk all the way to the gate. He looked around the deserted bridge.

Five hundred yards away, the new causeway was busy with evening traffic. The old bridge was empty, except for a few fishermen they'd passed three-quarters of a mile back.

"Where is she?"

"Out at the end. She promised she wouldn't do anything until I got back."

Cole agilely climbed the eight-foot wooden barrier. Armond followed him over. The strip of asphalt was deserted. The only sounds were the cries of seabirds.

Armond turned to Cole. "Damn. You don't think she . . . ?" He stopped talking.

The boy didn't look scared or worried anymore. The wolf's glare was back in his eyes. That, and unbridled rage and menace made Armond take a step back.

"What the fuck is going on, boy? You fuckin' got me way out here on some kind of bullshit?"

Cole's voice was soft. "No bullshit, man. You here to pay for fucking over my girl Taneesha."

Before Armond could even begin to respond, Cole's right hand flashed. Armond screamed, and both hands went to his face. Blood poured through his fingers. Cole had sliced his cheek open from just below his right eye to his chin.

Like a striking snake, Cole's hand flashed again and again. Wounds sprouted all over Armond's face and torso. He retreated from the pain all the way to the wooden barrier. Cole's attack had been so sudden and violent, he'd had no chance.

When Cole stepped back, the entire front of Armond's

body was a red mess. It took a while for him to realize no new cuts were being inflicted. He shook his head violently to clear his eyes of blood.

The barrel of the gun Cole was holding looked like a cannon.

"Yo, youngster, you gon' kill me over a bitch?"

Again Cole's voice was soft. "No. I'm doing it because you hurt my friend."

The two gunshots followed one another immediately. Armond crashed into the wooden gate then collapsed to the pavement. It was only a moment's work for Cole to roll his body into the bay.

He never talked about Armond to Sugar or the girls, not even Taneesha. They all guessed correctly at what had happened. By unspoken agreement, the subject never came up.

Cole had long ago lost count of the number of men he'd killed. He knew that he was missing something. Conscience, he supposed. Once he determined that death was called for, he never lost sleep or had a second thought about dealing it.

Chapter Thirteen

Sugar was having a rough day. His strenuous bouts with Taneesha, Mary, and Jessica the night before had him ragged this morning. He made a resolution to spread out the schedule with the girls. The "talk" sessions always seemed to end up with him fucking too.

Just before the lunch rush, he got a call from Shay. He had her and Alana for tonight. Then he had two days off from the girls.

Shay's message was short and to the point: "Hey, baby. Grease that dick up for me. I'll be by about seven-thirty. I got yours, so make sure you got mine. Bye!"

Sugar had to smile. Shay was certainly the least complicated of his women. She was the rare exception. A prostitute who whored for no other reason than that she wanted to. It stood to reason. She was a certified nymphomaniac.

Shay was black as coal. Slim, but fine. Big, juicy lips and a beautiful smile. She had come to work for the whorehouse just before it got closed down. She hadn't grown up with Sugar, Cole, and the girls, but with her easygoing, live-and-let-live attitude, she fit right in. She was from Hattiesburg, an hour or so north of the coast.

The story was, from the age of twelve, she couldn't stop fucking. Young, old, handsome, ugly—if it walked on two legs and had a dick, Shay would fuck it. Her parents lived in fear, either of her getting pregnant or killed. Her mother's brother provided the only viable solution when she was sixteen.

"Girl, since you can't sit on that little pussy, you might as well get paid for it. You can have unlimited dick, an' money too. I know a lady in Biloxi that'll be glad to have you."

That's how she got to the coast and into their lives. She'd chased Sugar around for a couple of years after she overheard Alana talking about how big his dick was. He ignored her. After the house got shut down, Shay continued sellin' herself out of her apartment.

One night, she heard Taneesha, Alana, Jessica, and Mary at a party, joking about their little game with Sugar. How they left him envelopes of money after he fucked them. They laughed about how they got the best of the deal, how much better he fucked than their men.

That did it for Shay. She confronted them and told them that either she got to play Sugar's Game, or everybody would hear about it. When they told Sugar, he agreed to meet with her, with the idea of talking her out of it, even if he had to fuck her.

When she walked into the room with him, she immediately jumped him.

"I been waitin' six years for this," she muttered as she tore at his clothes. "I want it now."

Before he knew what was happening, she had swallowed his dick. All of it. Nobody had ever been able to do that before. She nibbled at his nuts, his asshole, all the while pulling at him like she had a Hoover in her throat.

When he came, she swallowed and hummed at the same time. She took off her clothes and lay on the bed, ignoring him. Her little apple-size tits had long nipples, and when she spread her legs, her slit glowed bright pink amid the darkness of her skin. It was intensely erotic, and Sugar got hard again immediately.

Removing the rest of his clothes, he joined her. She raised her legs, wrapped them around his back, and pulled at his hips. He slid into her. She began to move. She moved sideways, back and forth, groaning and moaning all the time. He tried to set the pace but she was like a whirlwind.

Her pussy was sopping wet. Finally, he rose to his knees, took her thighs in his hands, and started to slam her down on his dick. He fucked her rough and deep. It was exactly what she wanted.

"Like that, Sugar. I know it. I know. Give it to me. More."

They went at it like two big cats. She clawed and bit, and he practically chewed her nipples off. Their mutual explosion seemed like a bomb blast.

Shay got up first and headed to the bathroom. Watching her ass twitch, Sugar felt his dick stir again.

"Damn," he muttered.

He bent her over the sink and fucked her from behind. He screwed her in the shower. When she got ready to go, she handed him an envelope.

"I don't think this is enough. This is the only time in my life I had enough dick in one night. Thank you."

She left him standing with his mouth open and his dick sore. Shay was the most purely sexual creature he'd ever known.

While he was standing there daydreaming, he nearly burned up a thousand dollars worth of meat. Mack was looking at him funny, and he was trying to hide a hard-on. He would be ready for Shay, but he had to save some for Alana.

She'd called too, and there was something in her voice that he couldn't figure out. How could a person sound happy and sad at the same time? Nora seemed to be acting strange too. He'd still catch her giving him funny looks.

Of all his girls, Shay, the freakiest of them all, seemed to be the only one acting normal. Or maybe he was just tired. He was young and strong, but he'd been at this for years. He wished Cole would come home.

Alana sat alone in her bedroom. The day had been hectic. Cisco had spent much of the day taking care of business. He'd been seeing people most of the night. He'd left the wedding and travel plans up to her.

She agonized a long time about whether or not to tell him about the girls and Sugar. She finally decided not to. She wasn't worried for herself. If she came clean, one of them would be hurt. Physically. She couldn't stand the thought.

She wouldn't just run out on Sugar either. Him, she could tell the truth. They had so much history together. He deserved a proper good-bye. Most of all she needed to talk to Jessica. If anybody could help Alana's confusion, it was Jessica. Hell, Jessica was the one who was really hung up on Sugar. Alana reached for the phone.

Chapter Fourteen

Bullet was in a foul mood all day. He'd followed through on his plan to go home and fuck Jessica the night before, but the encounter wasn't as satisfying as usual. He liked it when she twisted and moaned and told him how good he was.

Last night she'd seemed listless. Like she wasn't really into it. A kernel of self-doubt about his prowess had crept into his thoughts. That was unusual for him. He prided himself on the fact that he didn't need to eat pussy to satisfy a woman. All he had to do was lay pipe. None of them had ever complained. It never occurred to him that none of them were ever satisfied.

This morning, he had to roust her out of bed and send her out for breakfast. The ruse was necessary so he could hide the money he'd collected last night in his secret spot. He only kept it in the house until enough accumulated to make a boat ride to his bank necessary. Even Jessica didn't know where he kept it. At least, that's what he told himself.

Later, right before he left, Jessica received a phone call

at the house number. She took the mobile phone and walked out on the patio, speaking lowly and urgently. Fifteen minutes later, she came back inside. After she hung up, she turned to him.

"That was Alana. She said to tell you that Cisco said he needed to talk to you tonight. Something about some major changes. Anyway, she's coming over to visit me about nine o'clock this evening."

Something about her demeanor told him she wasn't telling all she knew. Bullet walked over to the phone as if to use it, but he really wanted to check the caller ID. Yeah, it was Cisco's regular house phone. He left, still wondering what the fuck was up.

He drove across the bay, and when he rolled up to the corner of Jefferson and Peyton, he saw an argument in progress. Pee-Wee, one of his dealers, was shouting at a dopehead about being short on his money.

Just what he needed, considering his mood. Stuffing his gun behind his back, he got out of his truck. He managed to remain unnoticed by the two men until he was right up on them. He pushed Pee-Wee out of the way and lit into the other guy.

Bullet was strong, and he could fight. He beat the shit out of the guy, ignoring the pleas and cries. When he lay bleeding at his feet, he grabbed him by the throat.

"Nigga, have my money in one hour. Pee-Wee tell me you don't, this ass-kicking won't seem like nothin'! You hear me?"

When he let go, the dude nodded, scrambling away from him until he could stand and stagger off.

Bullet gave Pee-Wee some dap and strolled back to his vehicle. He felt better, but not by much. Something was eating at him and he couldn't quite put his finger on it. He needed to burn off his bad mood. He had an idea.

Driving the short distance to Nixon Street, he pulled

up in front of his main dope house and leaned on his horn. A minute or so later, Ace opened the door.

"Come here," Bullet yelled from the truck.

Ace ambled over. "What's up, Big Dog?"

"'Member you told me the other day about them youngsters selling out of that house on Fallo?"

"Yeah. You said leave 'em alone. We'd take care of it later."

"Well, later is right now. Leave Brew in charge. Get Trey, that nigga Conch, and yourself ready. Strap up good and I'll be back in twenty minutes. Load up the Suburban. We gonna take a ride."

Ace nodded and turned to go back inside. Bullet backed out and drove over to Keller. He bought a bottle of peppermint schnapps and drove to Main and Murray and over to the park. He removed a flat, leather kit from inside his door panel. Laying out two thick lines of white powder, he snorted them and downed a healthy slug of the strong liquor, drinking from the bottle.

The crank slammed into him, and the schnapps burned into his stomach. Bullet didn't do cocaine, and he rarely did crystal meth. He usually stuck to liquor and lean. Today, the speed rush was just what he needed. Suddenly, he felt invincible. Jessica, Cisco, all of his nagging worries seemed like nothing. Time to kick ass and take names.

He replaced the kit and drove down Elmer to Baptist Lane, and in behind the dope house. A blue Suburban with three men in it was idling on the street. Bullet parked the Navigator and got into the passenger seat.

"You bring my street sweeper?"

"You know I did." Ace smiled, knowing how much his boss liked the deadly weapon.

"Let's do it. These young niggas got to learn not to disrespect a playa."

"No shit," said Conch from the backseat. His face was still swollen and his body ached from the beating Bullet had given him last night, but he was glad to have this chance to make it up.

The tension was high in the 'Burban. These were just rooty-poot young slingers, but they were surely packing. Bullets didn't give a fuck who they hit. Bullet passed around the schnapps, and it took the edge off. He still felt like Superman, and by the time they pulled up on Fallo, they were all ready.

The house was an old ranch-style, located just where Fallo Street curved south. Its grass was uncut in the small yard, and there wasn't another residence within thirty or forty yards. The place looked like it wouldn't be standing for long.

"Ace, you and Trey sneak around back. I'm-a give you ten minutes to get ready. Me and Conch goin' in the front. Try not to kill the cocksuckers. We really don't need no more heat. Go on."

Trey and Ace crouched and walked into the undergrowth on the near side of the house. Ace's little Uzi looked like a toy, but Trey's AK looked like what it was. In the truck Bullet jacked a round into the Cobra's chamber.

"What you packing, Conch?"

"I got that ten you got for me last month."

"You scared?"

"No. Not much."

Bullet smiled. "Let's go."

They got out of the truck and walked quickly up the overgrown walkway. Bullet didn't even pause. He raised his foot and kicked the wooden door. The lock sprung, but it remained closed. His second kick threw it wide open.

BOOM!

Bullet cut loose into the ceiling while shouting, "Police! Nobody move!"

Two guys were sitting at a table in the front room. One was still in the act of cutting up crack on a plate. The other was reaching for a gun lying on the table. At Bullet's shout, he looked up into the huge opening of the shotgun, still trailing smoke.

From the corner of his eye, Bullet saw Trey and Ace come through the kitchen and head down the hall leading to the rear of the house. There was a female scream, followed by a short burst from the Uzi. Then silence.

Shit, thought Bullet, really wired now.

"You two, move to the middle of the floor. Lie face down with your hands on your heads. Move and I'll blow holes in yo' bitch asses."

When the men complied, he motioned to Conch. "Go back and see what's up. Bring everybody up here."

Conch quickly moved to do as he was told. A couple of minutes later, two terrified young girls preceded the three men into the front room.

"Sit down and shut up." Bullet pointed to the two chairs vacated by the men on the floor.

"Now, I need to know who runs this house." He was watching the women. Neither spoke, but both sets of eyes flicked to the man nearest him.

Bullet looked at Ace. "Watch him." He pointed to the other youth. "What's your name?"

The kid lifted his face from the floor. Staring down the barrel of Bullet's gun, he looked scared but defiant. He said nothing. Neither did Bullet. He took one step and kicked the man in his side. The soft *crack* indicated the broken ribs. The boy screamed and curled up.

The cute girl with braids shouted, "Richard! He's Richard. Please don't hurt him no more!"

Bullet looked down at the kid writhing and moaning in pain. "You know who I am?"

Through gritted teeth, Richard muttered, "Yeah. You that nigga Bullet."

Scowling, Bullet couldn't help but admire the boy's guts. *I'd better watch him. He ain't broke yet*," he thought.

"Then don't you know nobody sell rock on this side of the bay 'less I say so? I'm gonna let you live this time. Yo' boy and you hoes too. For that I want your dope an' your money. Now."

Richard had started to shake his head when the other man spoke up.

"Fuck that, man. This shit ain't worth dyin' for. Don't you know this dude will kill us all?" He looked up at Bullet. "I'll give you the shit and the money. Y'all gonna let us make it? We won't sling here no more."

Bullet thought hard. The boy Richard still needed a lesson. He pointed to the girl with the braids.

"You, go get all the dope and all the money and bring it here. Conch, go with her. Trey, check outside and bring those tie wraps from the glove box."

Trey got back first. Bullet had him tie both men's hands with the cable ties. Richard moaned when his arms were pulled behind him. A couple of minutes later, Conch and the girl returned. They dropped a bread bag full of one-ounce cookies of crack, and three bundles of money on the table.

"Conch, you a boy who likes pussy. You and Trey take these two bitches to the back and fuck 'em." He looked at the girl with the braids. "If you two don't act nice to my boys, Richard and this one will be riding wheelchairs for the next fifty years. Understand?"

She hung her head. Tears flowed as Conch grabbed a handful of ass and guided her to the rear. Trey pushed the other girl ahead of him. Bullet sat and watched Richard as his eyes cycled from rage to hopeless despair as the sounds of sex came from the back room. When the two men came back up front straightening their clothes, Bullet rose.

"Remember—don't fuck with me. You' got off light. I can take your life and your mama's life just as easy as my boys took your pussy. Don't let me see you around here again."

Taking the money and stash, the four men left. Bullet was smiling. He felt a lot better.

Chapter Fifteen

Elnora wasn't having a good day either. Not many people, though, shared her idea of what a good day was. She lived in a perpetual fog. And she liked it that way. Her one lodestone, her focal point in life, was Sugar.

When he nearly burned up the meat, she knew something was bothering him. She didn't question him about it. That wasn't her way. Instead, she watched him, his facial expressions, his body language. Whatever it was, it had to do with one or more of the girls—with his Game.

Nora didn't know how she felt about The Game. She didn't allow herself to think like that. In fact, she had become adept at preventing herself from thinking about, or feeling much of anything except concern for, and protectiveness of, Sugar. The Game was what Sugar wanted to do. She would help in any way she could.

The girls all treated her like a retarded little sister. That was fine with her. Long ago, when she had first been brought to live with them, there'd been resentment. The girls had all assumed that Sugar's solicitousness and fierce protectiveness of her meant that he had emotional ties with her.

Later, after she had recovered from her injuries, they saw things differently. She went out of her way to make herself look plain and unattractive. She did the housework and most menial chores with humility and downcast eyes. She almost never spoke, except to Sugar.

It was Jessica who finally relented and made the others leave her alone. The questions and insinuations about Nora and Sugar finally stopped. Eventually they all accepted her as she was. Mostly, they treated like she wasn't even there.

At first, she panicked whenever Sugar was out of her sight. Gradually, with extreme patience, he got her to the point where she could function around other people. Then it got simpler for him. He snapped to the fact that she would do or attempt to do anything for him.

Sugar, slowly, carefully, drew her out of her shell. His only mistake was trying to get her to talk about her life before he'd found her. Her panic attack was so severe that he and the girls almost called 9-1-1.

She screamed and clawed her way past their attempts to restrain her, and into a closet. There she sat, wild-eyed and babbling for hours. She even fouled herself. The stink was bad. Sugar made everyone leave the room. When she finally wore herself out, he approached her talking softly.

Her eyes cleared and he could see recognition in them. Sugar called for Jessica to crush up two Valiums and dissolve them in a glass of orange juice. He coaxed Nora into drinking it down and sat on his heels with her, ignoring the smell until she passed out.

He cleaned her up and dressed her, holding her limp, naked body in his arms. Despite her lush beauty, without

the usual "disguise," he didn't feel arousal. He felt compassion, pain, and anger. She clung to him, whimpering
in her sleep until the next day.

From that day on, he let no one interfere with the way
she handled her trauma. If you wanted to really piss
Sugar off, fuck with Elnora. Even now, all these years
later, she would occasionally, after a particularly bad
nightmare, come to his bed. Her terror didn't allow her
to notice his tenseness and arousal as he held and com-
forted her.

To almost everyone else, she was just plain, queer Elnora. There was much speculation as to whether she was
Sugar's woman, his sister, or what. Asking him usually
got your head bit off.

Nora's peculiar behavior led people to believe that she
was slightly retarded. Her competence in cooking the food
and running the restaurant as well as Sugar's home was
treated as learned behavior. They couldn't have been more
wrong. This was good for her, for she would need all her
intelligence to handle what was happening to her.

Her lousy day wasn't just due to her concern for Sugar.
Nora's internal walls were starting to crumble. Usually
her thoughts were either stark terror or a calm fog with
Sugar at its center. Lately, though, she'd been having
thoughts about him that were alien to her. For the first
time in her post-trauma memory, she felt something
missing, even (or especially) when Sugar was around. It
bothered her. And she was beginning to not like Sugar's
Game very much.

Chapter Sixteen

Shay blew into the room like a slim, black hurricane. As usual, she attacked right off. Sugar had learned long ago not to wear much clothing when he was expecting her. She had almost torn his dick off once trying to get it out.

She pushed him onto the bed and crammed most of him into her hot mouth, when she suddenly stopped.

"Uh-uh, Sugar. None of this shit. Not on my day. I came to get mine. Now what the fuck is wrong?"

Shay was much more perceptive than he'd given her credit for. Right off she'd seen his preoccupation. Looking at her, his dick lying against her cheek, titties falling out of her tank top, just oozing sex, he had to smile.

Reaching down, he pulled her up his body. Flipping her slight form over onto her back, he twisted himself and pinned her to the bed with his body. Raising her top, he took one long nipple into his mouth and sucked, feeling it lengthen even more.

He knew she didn't wear panties under the short skirt.

He pushed her up and pried her thighs apart with his knee.

"So you want yours, huh? Okay."

He rammed his dick into her. As his rod stretched her pussy, she clawed at his back and bucked her hips.

"Aaaah. That's it. Fuck me. Mama gon' make you forget everything but her."

Shay tossed her head in ecstasy and proceeded to keep her word. Her hot pussy pulled at his dick. She undulated her body, wrapping her arms and legs around him and working her hips like a jackhammer. As always, Sugar got caught up in the fucking/fighting madness she brought on.

He didn't remember consciously changing positions, but he was pounding into her from behind, making her tear at the sheets as he drove in and out of her body. Somehow she got astride him, riding his dick with abandon.

They were in this position when she started to tremble. Shay sat down hard, taking all of him in. Her pussy started to leak hot juices as it clutched at his dick in orgasm. His groin was flooded with her issue.

Sugar rolled her off him. She lay gasping on her side when he eased up behind her. Taking her in his arms, he spooned her, his hard dick pressing against her ass. Sliding down in the bed a little, he adjusted the angle so he could enter again.

"Oh, you cheated, baby. You didn't come. Give me a minute and I'll fix that."

She started to push back against him. Each time her soft ass met his groin, he seemed to get harder. When she started to move faster, and he sensed she was about to start wildly humping him again, he hugged her tightly to him, one breast in each hand, and threw his leg across her hips.

Sugar continued to stroke in and out of her slowly. Her movements were inhibited by his weight. It felt good, but she wanted to fuck.

"You know, Shay, I fuck a lot of women. They are all fine and beautiful, and the pussy is great."

They rocked together. His soft voice and the wet, sucking sound of his dick in her were the only sounds.

"But you, you are the hottest woman I've ever had. I don't care what else is going on, when I see you, when I think about you, my dick gets hard and I want to fuck. Sometimes it seems like we're trying to kill each other, but what a way to die."

Sugar started moving faster, going deeper with each thrust. He rolled her over onto her stomach, still joined to her. Fucking her all the while, he did his thing with the pillows, stuffing them under her belly. He opened his legs wide, so that both of hers were contained within his, his legs twining around hers.

"I like fucking you so much, I'd pay you. I even let you have it your way every time." His voice got even softer. "Right now, though, we gonna do this Sugar's way."

He started to pump into her, his groin slamming against her ass. Shay couldn't move much, new territory for her, so she closed her eyes and reveled in the sensations. Sugar's hands pinching her aching nipples. His big dick ramming deep into her pussy. How wet her ass was with sweat and cum, so that his skin slid against hers every time they touched.

She pushed back against him as best she could, wanting more, even though the depth and force of his thrusts were already hurting a little. Sugar's breathing quickened, and she could feel him swell inside her, stretching her even further.

Shay forced her hand under her body, working her clit. She knew he was almost there, and she wanted to be with him. He held tightly to her with his last stroke, and just as she felt his hot seed deep within her, she went over the top.

Even with his weight pinning her, Sugar could feel her ass flexing as her pussy milked him. They strained against each other for another minute. Then he rolled off her.

When Shay came out of the restroom from cleaning up, she was uncharacteristically quiet. Sugar was even more amazed when, as she kneeled to kiss him softly on the lips, he saw her eyes were wet. She laid an envelope by his head and left, softly closing the door.

As Sugar came back into the room from the shower, he was debating within himself whether to eat now or later. He started when he saw the shadow by the window. It was Nora. She stood, holding the envelope, eyes fixed on the night sky.

Hearing his step, she turned. Her eyes flicked to the towel around his waist, and it seemed to him, even in the low light, that she flushed.

"Shay may not be back. She said nothing's wrong, but you're taking her places she's not sure she's ready to go yet. And she said to tell you thank you."

"Damn, Nora. What's happening? I don't know about Taneesha, Mary and Jessica are acting weird, and something's up with Alana. What's wrong?"

To his intense surprise, she answered. He had become so used to using her as his sounding board, and her corresponding with gentle, placating answers, he had almost forgotten she was the one person who knew all his business.

"Taneesha wants to go to San Francisco. Mary Jane is ready to just stay home. Alana is getting married and leaving the country with Cisco."

Sugar's shock deepened. In just a couple of sentences, she had revealed a wealth of information.

"And what about Jess?"

"Jessica thinks she loves you. She knows you don't love her, but she doesn't know she doesn't love you either."

"And you?"

"Me?" Her face got redder.

"Yeah, you. What about you?"

"I'll always be with you."

She said this softly, without meeting his eyes. Then she quickly left the room.

CHAPTER SEVENTEEN

Sugar sat in the bedroom armchair waiting for Alana. The revelations Elnora had delivered an hour earlier chased themselves through his brain. Taneesha and Alana leaving town. Shay not coming back to him. Mary dissatisfied. Jessica was the only one who seemed stable. Well, who seemed the same anyway.

And Nora. She definitely seemed different. When had all his girls started to change? He prided himself not just on the fact that he was satisfying them sexually and getting paid for it, but that he cared for them in other ways too. He always had. They and Cole had always seemed more like family than just good friends.

The truth he was arriving at in his thoughts wasn't very appetizing. He'd become selfish and arrogant. His concern used to be almost totally for them and their needs. Especially Nora. Now that his business was an unqualified success and the girls had financial security and didn't have to prostitute themselves, he seemed more focused on sex and money than the women themselves.

Had he changed so much? Was it all going to his head as it did to so many others? He'd derided the dealers and hustlers who amassed fortunes. The six-figure cars, world-class mansions, and power-drunk lifestyles. Wasn't he becoming just like them, or worse?

They at least had the excuse that most of the women they were using were using them too. For the money and lifestyle. But his girls were his friends. From childhood. They depended on him for a lot more than just sex. He was beginning to feel that he had let them down. And himself.

His dark, brooding mood was interrupted by the arrival of Alana. Nora quietly ushered her in then left, closing the door behind her. Alana looked at him calmly for a minute. Then she walked to the dresser and placed something on it, setting her purse down.

Coming over to sit beside him, she spoke for the first time. "Hey, Sugar."

"Hey, baby."

"You know, don't you? About me and Cisco, and about our leaving?"

"Yeah."

"Are you mad? Disappointed in me?"

"Nah, girl. Let me ask you something. Truth. Are you happy?"

"Yeah. I think so. No. I know so. Sugar, I don't know when I figured out I really love him. He's not what I thought. I guess we both been dodging the issue. He wants to get out of the business and leave. I want that too."

"Does he know about us? The Game and everything?"

"No, and I'm not gonna tell him. He wouldn't be able to handle it. I mean, who would really understand about us? About all of us? You're our friend, lover, father, brother, protector, and you always been those things to us."

She got up from her seat and walked over to him. She sat in his lap.

"Sugar, you always will be all of that to me. I know you don't care about or need the money. We could stop that. But if I stay here, I'll always come to you sometimes. Even if we never get caught, the guilt would eat me up. You see?"

She asked this with a yearning in her voice. It was important to her that he understand. He could tell.

"You know I do. Lana, you know none of you never have been whores to me. I've been thinkin'. I want you to be happy, to have a full life. I wish you and Cisco good luck, lots of babies, and long lives. I mean it."

"Oh, Sugar."

The tears came then. She lay her head on his chest and cried. He stroked her back and shushed her. After a couple of minutes, the sobs stopped. She raised her tear-stained face to his and kissed him softly. Her tongue probed his lips until his mouth opened. The kiss deepened. She rotated her ass slowly in his lap. He broke the kiss.

"Lana."

"Ssshh. Let's say good-bye this way. I really, really want to." Her hand found his stiffening dick through his robe. "And you know you do too."

She stood to take off her clothes. When she was naked before him, Sugar bit back the J-Lo comment that rose in his thoughts. Alana was truly beautiful. The thick patch of hair between her legs glistened with moisture. He remembered the salty, tangy taste of her. He wanted to experience it once more.

Kneeling on the floor, Sugar filled his hands with her big, soft ass. He bent his head forward and licked her, burrowing through her bush to the slit beneath. He ran his tongue up her pussy, licking the little bud at the top with its tip. She moaned.

"Aaah. Sugar."

He squeezed her ass. Turning her, he pushed her down into the chair he'd vacated. Pulling so that her ass was on the very edge, he raised her legs and tipped her backward. Then he went to work on her with his mouth.

For a while, he slid his tongue in and out of her opening. He knew she liked that. When her movements got frantic, he took his thumb and slid back the sheath covering her clitoris. He licked it lightly, very fast, as he worked the finger of his other hand into her.

Alana came with a shout. The feel of her pussy clamping down on his finger made his dick throb painfully. When her spasms died away, he stood. She reached for his dick and started to suck greedily on the head.

"Uh-uh. Later for that. Come on."

He withdrew himself from her mouth and raised her to her feet. Sugar bent her over the padded arm of the chair. He admired the huge, pale globes of her ass. Impatient now, he prodded between them with his dick. He let out a deep sigh as he sunk slowly into her.

Sugar liked to do it doggie-style. It was one of his favorite positions. Nothing else had ever felt like pushing against Alana's ass from behind, though. The J-Lo comparison was apt. The butt was big. He pumped into her, lost in the sensation.

Alana pushed back against him as best she could. His big strong hands on the top of her hips controlled the action. It seemed to her as if each stroke hit her harder, went deeper. The only thing in the world she wanted right now was for Sugar to keep driving into her.

When she heard him moan, she knew he was close. Bending her knees slightly, she worked her ass up and down, his grip on her slackening as she flattened her cheeks against him, taking him deeper still. It had the desired effect.

Neither of them wanted to end it. For the next hour and a half, they showered, sucked, and fucked. When they were finally exhausted, Alana lay in his arms for the final time.

Sugar said, "I meant what I said earlier, baby. I'm happy for you. Just know that I'm always here for you. Don't forget Sugar."

Alana gave a bitter laugh. "After that fucking, I'll be lucky if I can leave for another week. Sugar, nothing could ever make me forget you. My first son's name will be Jameel."

They talked awhile, each reluctant to acknowledge that it was time. There was a gentle knock on the door.

"Elnora says it's time," Sugar said.

"I know. Sugar, take care of her. She's different, somehow. More there. Watch her, hear?"

She got dressed and walked out of his life. He felt that he'd lost a part of himself. He drifted off to sleep with her taste, her smell all over him.

Chapter Eighteen

Alana knew she was running late. She seldom looked or felt as disheveled as she did now. Her hair and clothes were a mess as she climbed into Jessica's Lexus. Automatically, she straightened her clothes, hair, and makeup as she drove.

Tears filled her eyes as the full realization hit her that she had been intimate with Sugar for the last time. The sex had been over the top, as always. Her pussy had that pleasant soreness that signaled physical satisfaction.

It wasn't the loss of that sweet dick that brought the tears, though. It was the knowledge that a very major turning point in her life had been reached.

Cisco satisfied her physically. That was a fact.

With Sugar, though, there was that intangible something else. The feeling of complete relaxation and acceptance. She could lay all her pain, worries, and insecurity at his feet and know that he would understand. Completely.

That was irreplaceable. She could only pray that in time the love between herself and Cisco would mature into the total trust and friendship that was the basis for all strong relationships. And truth be told, she would miss the dick.

Alana let her mind wander back almost twenty years and a couple of miles to the whorehouse where she was raised. Lost in memory, she didn't notice the Navigator that sat through its green light at Atkison Road and Creek. If she had, things might have turned out differently.

Her mother Maria had been one of the working girls at Berea's house. She had been a beauty, and most of Alana's looks (and that amazing ass) came from her. Maria had migrated to Biloxi from Baltimore, following an airman she thought loved her.

When she became pregnant with Alana and he received a transfer, he left her. Destitute and almost broke, Maria managed to work domestic jobs until Alana was born. Then things got really bad.

She'd had to resort to being kept by a series of military men for a few years. Her pride wouldn't let her return to B'more with a baby and no husband and have to submit to a lifetime of "I told you so" from her family.

After she met Berea by accident, it didn't take long for her to become sold on the idea of a permanent place to live, security and companionship for her baby, and a steady, plentiful source of income. So what if it was a whorehouse?

What she was doing now wasn't much better, and with these fickle-ass soldiers, or airmen—whatever—there sure was no future in it. So she went for Berea's deal.

The third floor of the house had apartments set up for some of the working girls. Of course, Berea charged them rent. Maria and Alana's apartment was next door to Mary's.

Several of Berea's girls had children of various ages,

but by the end of third or fourth grade, Alana's group of friends was set for life.

There was outspoken, confident, bossy Jessica; quiet, sensible, dependable Mary Jane (a.k.a. M.J.); Taneesha, reserved and somehow twisted; and herself. Big-butt Alana. Often mistaken for Black. Shit, Jessica and, certainly, Taneesha had a lighter skin color than hers. And when they were very young, there didn't seem to be so many Hispanics around.

Then there was Cole. Sexy and dangerous. Trouble and violence seemed to live in his quiet eyes. And Sugar. Strong, gentle, and smart.

Alana and her friends were a close-knit group. They were nearly always together. Looking out for each other was a way of life. Prostitutes didn't always make the best mothers. No matter. They had each other.

Often, Alana had wondered what would have happened if they had all managed to stay together until adulthood. No doubt she, Jessica, Taneesha, and Mary would not have become hookers. Sugar and Cole wouldn't have stood for it.

The point was moot, though. During their mid-teens all their lives changed, seemingly overnight. Sugar got sent to reform school, and Cole left town one step ahead of the law. The girls lost both their protectors at once.

Taneesha and Jessica got sent across the bay to another house. In other words, their mothers decided it was time for them to start whoring for a living, and at a place where their beauty wouldn't compete with that of the women who birthed them.

Things were a little different for Alana and Mary. The pressure came mostly from Berea. A trick had raped Jessica, but this didn't occur often. Reuben didn't play that shit. He was powerless to intervene this time, though. Sugar may have been able to, but he was gone.

As usual, it all came down to money. Berea took a page from the old-time New Orleans Fancy House. She auctioned off their cherries. For a shitload of cash.

The way it worked in Storyville, the old red-light district in New Orleans, when the young, light-skinned girls came of age, they threw a big fancy party called The Quadroon Ball.

Young, rich, White plantation owners would bid for, or make a contract with, the girls' mothers for their virginity, or the chance to make them their *placeés,* which was a fancy word for *mistresses*. The sums paid were huge.

How Berea found out about this custom, Alana never knew, but she became, along with Mary, a victim of the modern-day version of it.

Calling a meeting of the richest customers of her house, Berea laid out the deal. She had two beautiful sixteen-year-old virgins who would soon be working her house. The men who bid the most money would be the ones to break them in. To up the ante, she paraded Alana and Mary, in Victoria's Secret, naturally, before them.

Of course the girls had tried to rebel. Between Berea, their mothers, and the possibility of being put out to hustle the streets for peanuts, they were talked into it. The huge sums of money they were promised helped, along with the fact that Sugar, Cole, Jessica, and Taneesha were gone.

Alana and Mary looked good. Young, fine, and beautiful, the sexy lingerie set them off. The dozen or so men, most of them old and White, went wild. Mary's cherry went for eight grand and Alana's for eleven.

The hot tea laced with roofies (date rape pills) that Reuben gave them made the first time bearable. Alana and Mary never really remembered it. The tricks were happy, though.

Over the course of the next few months, the girls became professional prostitutes.

Berea was happy, their mothers were happy, and they were miserable. Alana's biggest fear was that her high school classmates would find out that, on nights after school, she spread her legs for a living. Mary just stayed high. They tried to encourage and support each other, but it was hard.

Then Sugar came back. Alana and Mary were so happy to see him, they almost shit. Sugar wasn't so happy, though. Seeing his friends whoring for a living pissed him off.

He and Berea had a big fight. Sugar threatened to take all four girls and leave. Berea called him an ungrateful bastard. Reuben and Tichi had to separate them.

Then the new mayor took office, and with him came crackdowns.

Berea had ample warning that the house had to shut down, maybe permanently. Sugar's threat now became a necessity. He took the girls with him and rented an old warehouse on the docks. He took care of them all.

Alana's musings had brought her all the way to Jessica and Bullet's house. Sighing deeply at the knowledge that she was leaving her "peeps," she went inside.

CHAPTER NINETEEN

Bullet's last stop for the night was in Hiller Park. He had to drop off an ounce of powder to this technical sergeant from the Air Force base. The violence from earlier, not to mention the crank and lean, had worn off and 1eft him tired. He decided to go home and rest before he saw Cisco.

Jessica had told him she expected a visit from Alana, and he wanted to see if she'd found out anything. Since he was on the western side of Keesler and Cisco lived clear on the eastern side of the base, it was not too long a trip to catch Atkinson Road out to Carter, cross the bay, drive to his house, and catch the 110 back across the water to Cisco's condo.

Just as he got to the stop light at Atkinson and Creek, he looked to his left. He did a double take. That was Jessica's Lexus! The woman driving wasn't Jessica, though. Even though the light was green for her, she sat fluffing her hair, applying lipstick, and straightening her clothes. When she moved through the intersection, not even glancing at the Navigator, he saw that it was Alana.

What the fuck is she doing here? And in my old lady's car?

His first thought was that Jessica had her following him. That couldn't be it. Then it hit him. That nigga from the barbecue place. Sugar. His house was at Creek and Hiller.

Damn! That ho Alana was fucking him.

He pulled out his cell and dialed home. Before Jessica answered, he hung up.

He followed the Lexus. Just as they crossed Jim Money Road, his phone rang. It was Jessica.

"Hey, baby. You just try to call me?"

"Yeah. I'm on my way in. Fix me a plate. Alana still there?"

"No. Her car messed up. I let her borrow mine. She was supposed to call AAA to come look at it. I don't know. I went to sleep. Let me go heat your dinner. Bye."

So that was it. Still, he believed Jessica knew her friend was cheating with Sugar. Who'd have thought? That nigga wasn't no more than a mark. A sugar daddy. Bullet wouldn't have figured him to have the nuts to mess with Cisco's property. Wait till later on.

When Alana pulled into his driveway, Bullet hung back. She parked the white Lexus next to her own Benz. When Jessica let her in, Bullet pulled down the street and parked behind Alana's car. He got out and let himself in.

Jessica met him at the door. "Hi, baby."

She kissed his cheek.

"Alana just got back. I got your food almost ready. Go say hi. She's in the living room."

When Bullet entered the room, Alana was just hanging up the phone on the bar. She turned to him.

"Hi, Bullet. I was just talking to Cisco. He said to come on over after you eat. I had to go see my cousin. I'm gonna talk to Jess awhile, then go on home. It's almost midnight."

Uh-huh, thought Bullet, watching her closely. *She's been fucking. You can see it on her, the way she walks. No-good bitch. Fine as shit, though.*

Aloud he said, "No sweat. You and Jessica talk long as you want. You know what Cisco wants?"

"Yeah, but I don't get in his business. Let him tell you. It's good news, though."

Bullet left it at that. He went in to eat. Sitting alone at the table, he began to think. There was some strange shit going on. He decided he would sit on his little discovery about Alana until he needed it. If nothing else, he could force the little bitch to fuck him too.

Telling Cisco might cause more problems than it solved. The motherfucker was crazy. Sugar must be out of his mind. At least he didn't have to worry about his. No nigga had them kind of nuts.

When he stuck his head in to tell them he was leaving, they were huddled up on the sofa. Yep. Both them bitches were conniving. He'd have a serious talk with Jessica later. One thing for that ho Alana to be stepping out on his connection. A whole 'nother deal for his woman to be helping her. It might reflect back on him. He left.

Bullet chewed on the whole situation during the twenty minutes or so it took him to drive to Cisco's house. He was no genius, but he was as cunning as any savage animal. There were a multitude of ways this could play out. Stopping at the corner of Cisco's street, he checked the clip on his nine, then jacked a round into the chamber.

Chapter Twenty

Francisco sat back on his sofa. He heaved a sigh of satisfaction. Things were coming together perfectly. Once he made up his mind to do something, he didn't hesitate. The decision to get out had galvanized him into motion. In less time than he'd thought possible, his whole life had changed.

He and Jesse Verdun, his Rican homeboy from Gulfport, had virtually a lock on cocaine imports into Biloxi. They each had their territory, and didn't violate. Waveland, Bay St. Louis, Pass Christian, Long Beach, and Gulfport belonged to Jesse. Biloxi, Ocean Springs, Moss Point, and Pascagoula, to him. Wiggins, Hattiesburg, McComb, Tylertown, and the other small towns north of the coast were shared.

Today, Jesse got what he had always wanted. All of it. The Colombians who sent in the kilos didn't give a shit who ran what, just as long as the volume stayed up and the cash kept flowing.

Bullet and his other main middleman, T.C. from Pascagoula, would step up, and Jesse would supply them.

Cisco had spent most of the day with his people setting it up. He had also moved most of his money—millions—into his account in Belize. The three hundred thousand in cash from his wall safe was upstairs in a bag. Other than that, he and Alana would each take one suitcase. They were simply walking away from the house and everything else.

That dude Bullet was going to be blessed. His attitude had always irritated Cisco, but he always stacked paper. Shit, maybe he'd earned his shot at the next level. And if he fucked it up, then that wouldn't be Cisco's problem. Jesse had seemed really eager to have him. Well, him and all the rest, they were welcome to it.

The doorbell interrupted his thoughts.

"Bullet! Homie! Come on in."

"What's up, Cisco? Shit, it's quiet in here. This a bad time?"

"No, no. I need to talk business with you. My boys are gone. I don' need bodyguards to talk with my best customer. Alana is at your house. Come in and sit. Let me get you a drink."

Bullet was wary. This was a different Cisco from the one he usually saw. Since the Puerto Ricans had solidified their grip on the coast, things had settled down. But Bullet remembered when Cisco was a savage, ruthless drug lord, and he always had his crew strapped and loaded for bear around him.

Accepting his drink, Bullet spoke first. "Yeah, man, I need to talk to you too. I'm going to need more product. Damn near double. I hope I can get a break on the price too."

"Then, homes, you about to be one happy man. Starting tomorrow, you will have all the shit you want and more. This house, my rides, all will be yours. I'm leaving. Getting out of the business."

Bullet was thunderstruck. *What the fuck is he saying? Leaving? The house, cars, and dope? All his shit!*

"Where are you going?"

"Me an' Alana gonna move South and get married. Make babies. You're gon' be the man here now. I got it all set up. You'll see."

Bullet was starting to think again. This was too good to be true. If it was true, though, all his dreams were being handed to him. His mind was already awash with plans as to how he would change things.

"Congratulations, bro. But if you leave tomorrow, how am I gonna get my product? Directly from the boats?"

"No, those dudes won't deal with nobody new. My homie in North Gulfport will handle that part. I already tol' him. He say you know him. Jesse Verdun?"

The bottom dropped out of Bullet's world. Panic set in. *Fuck! Not that grease ball. No way!* he thought.

"Yeah, I know him," he said to Cisco. "Gimme a minute. I got to go piss."

He rose and headed for the toilet under the stairs, his mind awash with memories.

A few years ago, just when he had started buying multiple kilos from Cisco, he got a call from a friend in Gulfport. His friend had three dudes from Fayette who were looking to buy five birds at twenty-five gees each. They had the money. The deal between Jesse and Cisco was fairly new, but the profit margin drove Bullet to ignore that fact.

He had Ace step on the dope, wrapped up five keys, and met the guys from Fayette at a Gulfport club. After the deal went down, a black Escalade pulled up next to Bullet's ride in the parking lot. It was Jesse and a couple of Ricans from his crew.

Bullet had Ace, Trey, and Brew with him. Jesse, probably with the new truce with Cisco in mind, made the mistake of trying to be reasonable. Before he got far into his rap about his territory being violated, Bullet and his boys reacted.

While his boys disarmed and pistol-whipped Jesse's crew, Bullet beat the slim Rican damn near to death. Ace had to pull him off the dude. They loaded up and went back to Biloxi. With Ace prompting, Bullet did one of the few really smart things in his life.

He went straight to Cisco. He explained that the deal was with one of his old customers who'd moved north, and that these dudes fronted them and he thought it was a jack move. To top it off, he used a hundred grand to buy more birds right then.

It sold. Cisco went to North Gulfport and stood for Bullet and his boys. It was a mistake. The dudes didn't even know who Jesse was. If there was to be a beef, fine. If not, the original deal stood. No more violations. Laid up and not being entirely stupid, Jesse went along.

Nobody noticed when Bullet's boy who'd set the deal up disappeared. Jesse knew the whole score, but he just sat and bided his time. Now his time had come. Bullet knew that if Cisco left tomorrow morning, he'd be dead by tomorrow night. He couldn't win a war with Jesse without Cisco.

Bullet finished pissing into the toilet, flushed, and while he was washing his hands, staring into the mirror, the answer came to him. He knew how he could hold Cisco here at least long enough to figure out what to do. He opened the door and headed back into the living room.

Chapter Twenty-One

"Cisco, I really appreciate what you're doing for me. My boys are ready to step up. I been thinking, though. You been straight with me. I don' usually get in another man's business, but I found out somethin' tonight I think you ought to know. Before you take off with your girl."

"What?" Cisco eyes narrowed. He didn't know what Bullet was up to, but he'd been getting strange vibes from him ever since he came in. He casually strolled over the bar.

"I don't know how to tell you this, man, so I'm-a just say it. Your girl, Lana, she been fucking with that nigga Sugar, the one who runs that barbecue place over by the base. I saw her myself. Tonight."

Cisco whirled in his tracks, his eyes wide with shock. His mind flitted across the scene with Alana in bed this morning. He knew bullshit when he heard it. Alana had been for real. He was sure of it. This black-ass motherfucker was lying. Anger washed over him like a wave.

He turned back to the bar, reaching across it for his

gun. Fuck Bullet. Jesse could have it all. This nigga was playin' some kind of game. He didn't know who he was fucking with. Cisco's hand closed on the pistol grip, and he started to turn.

BAM! BAM!

Cisco's body jerked with the impact of the bullets. Mouth stretched open in shock, blood spurting from the two chest wounds, he was dead before his body rebounded off the bar and crumpled to the floor. The last sight his mind registered was Bullet's smoking gun.

Bullet himself had reacted without conscious thought. He had survived this long by being the first to strike, to wound, to kill. When he'd seen Cisco go for the gun, his reflexes had taken over. Now the shit had hit the fan for real. The killing didn't bother him. Hell, he'd lost count of the people he'd capped. He really didn't like the greasy asshole, anyway.

Still holding his piece, he backed to the sofa and sat. What the fuck to do now? He had to get the hell out of there, but right now he could only think of the financial implications of killing his golden goose.

He heard a slight sound and whirled. Alana stood there, her purse at her feet, both hands covering her mouth as if to stop the high, keening sound coming from within her. She wasn't looking at Bullet, but at Cisco lying in a widening pool of blood.

"No! Noooo!" she wailed as she ran to the body and threw herself upon it. "Baby, no!"

Bullet stood and walked toward her. "Bitch! You no-good whore! This shit is your fault. You was still putting your clothes back on when you was leaving that nigga's house. I saw you! I didn't know this weak-ass punk was goin' to try an' cap me when I tol' him about it."

Alana looked up at him, blinded by tears. His words filtered through her grief and struck her heart like a knife. Sugar! This asshole had seen her and told Cisco. She could guess the rest. His death was her fault.

"Now get your ass up and out of them clothes. Before I leave I want to see if that fine-ass pussy is good enough to die for. You need some real dick anyway. This pussy-ass Rican an' that limp-dicked nigga Sugar couldn't handle all that booty no how."

Alana snapped. She rose, spitting Spanish curses, almost unaware that she held Cisco's pistol. "*¡Pendejo! ¡Maricón!* Cisco was more man than you'll ever be! And Sugar? Limp dick? Ask your woman, every time you stick your little tiny dick in her, she has to run to Sugar to get some real meat. She pays for it with your money too. Fuck you!"

Even if she hadn't been bringing the gun up, her words cut so deep that Bullet probably would have done it anyway. He shot her. The bullet took her in the stomach, blowing her against the bar. He turned away before she even hit the floor, shaking with rage and humiliation.

Unlike Cisco, he instantly believed what Alana had said about Jessica. Lyin' ho. Playing him, huh? He'd deal with her first. Then that nigga Sugar. Jesse's bitch ass too. Then he'd have it all. He flipped open his cell phone as he climbed into this truck.

Chapter Twenty-Two

Alana's guts were on fire. She was dying. She knew it. Blood poured through the fingers she pressed against the hole in her belly. No matter. Cisco was dead. It was all her fault. She wished Jessica and Sugar were here. Her eyes snapped open. *Jess!*

She spotted her purse. It looked as if it were a thousand miles away. Slowly, she inched her way toward it. Each tiny movement brought waves of pain.

"Please. Please," she prayed. She was so afraid she would pass out before she got there. Faintly she heard the wail of sirens in the distance. She tried to move faster. Finally her fingers touched the cool leather. Tears of pain and grief flowed as she opened the purse. She found the phone and opened it by touch. Mustering her strength, she managed to punch the button for Jessica's pre-programmed number and send the call. It seemed like an eternity before her friend picked up.

"Hey, baby. You just left here. What did you forget?"

"Jess, listen, Cisco's dead. Bullet shot him. Me too. He knows about Sugar. Run. Call Cole, now. Bullet's gone . . ."

"Alana! Lana, please!"

The phone slipped from Alana's dead hand as police and paramedics burst through the door.

Bullet pulled over into a parking lot at the corner of Bayview and De Soto. He was snorting the first line of crystal from the stash in the truck's door when three Biloxi Police Department cruisers, sirens screaming, tore past him. *Fuck 'em,* he thought. The rush of the speed cleared his head. His mind clicked a mile a minute.

First, drive over to the 110 and across the back bay to the house. Take care of that bitch Jessica and get my money I keep stashed there.

Then he'd have to collect Ace and the boys he'd already put on point. *Go to North Gulfport and pay Jesse a surprise visit. In and out. Cap him and get in the wind.* By the time he got back, his boys would have that nigga Sugar and his girl Nora waiting for him. *See how that bitch-ass punk likes watching me and my boys pull a train on that little funny-acting retarded ho. Dust Sugar, and it'll be all over.*

It was gonna cost him a lot to grease the cops. But he had connections. When it was all over, he'd be the biggest dick left. It would all be his. Putting the Navigator in gear, he went to catch the freeway to his house.

Jessica was in a panic. The china cabinet was too heavy! She had to shift it. Her heart was thudding in her chest. Alana was dead. She had to lock away her grief, or she would be too. For once she was glad of her past. Her younger years had seen more than their share of drama and grief. And violence . . .

That nigga Bullet thought she had no idea of where he kept his money. She put one foot on the wall and wedged her fingers into the narrow gap between the heavy cabinet and the wall and heaved. No good. The answer came in a flash. She was so stupid. The damn thing was full.

In a frenzy, she ripped open the double doors. The expensive China and silver serving dishes made a horrendous noise as she desperately flung them across the dining room. When the shelves were empty, she pulled the drawers out and cast them aside.

When she pulled at the heavy piece of furniture this time, it slowly slid away from the wall. After the opening became wide enough, she squeezed in behind it and, bracing her back against the wall, pushed. It toppled over with a crash. The effort made her appreciate Bullet's immense physical strength.

Long ago, when he'd thought he'd sexed her into a sound sleep (as if he could), he had moved the cabinet away from the wall to access his "secret" spot. He had never noticed her peeping around the arched doorway. Now he would pay for his inattention. And a lot more.

Lifting the rug, she opened the recessed door. A large black leather bag rested there. She grunted as she lifted it out. Her jewelry box was in her purse. Throwing it over her shoulder, she dragged the bag to the garage door. She was taking nothing else. Except the account numbers to his offshore bank account.

After disconnecting with Alana, she had placed three quick phone calls. One to Houston and two here in Biloxi. Taking Bullet's money was the only deviation she would make to the instructions she'd received. Perversely, in spite of her grief, she felt a strange thrill at reliving the old sense of danger. And togetherness.

CHAPTER TWENTY-THREE

Cole pulled into the lot of the old Della Street Hotel in Houston. He parked next to a big yellow Hummer, and a big stocky Hispanic man got out of the passenger side. Cole met him between the vehicles.

"Jose. Long time, bro . . ."

The two men hugged.

"You bring the stuff I need? I've got to get on the road."

"*Sí*, I got it. You sure you don't need some help? My boys would be glad to go."

"Thanks, man. I better do this alone. It's family drama."

Jose opened the rear of the Hummer. "Everything you asked for. And this." He reached into his jacket and withdrew a thick envelope wrapped in rubber bands.

Cole took it and wedged it under his belt. "How much?"

"Sixty thousand. Call me and I'll wire more if you need it. It's all I had handy when you called. You said not to wait."

"No problem. Help me throw this shit in the truck."

In a couple of minutes, the heavy cargo was transferred.

"Try not to get stopped, *amigo*. That shit would get you Fed life."

"I know. I got to chance it. No time to do it any other way. My brother needs me."

"Well. *Vaya con Dios,* my friend. Let me know how it comes out."

"I will. Later, Jose."

Cole shut the trunk and climbed into the driver's seat. He took off, headed for the 110. Jessica's call had been urgent. Hearing her voice had stirred something in him. Right now, though, all he could think about was some nigga trying to cap Sugar. And Jess. Alana was dead.

This dude was supposed to be some kind of bad-ass with plenty of soldiers. A stone killer. Cole grinned. He hadn't met but a couple of *real* killers. Early tomorrow afternoon Cole would be in Biloxi. Then he'd show them bad-ass.

CHAPTER TWENTY-FOUR

Bullet frowned as the garage door rolled up. His black Lexus was there, but Jessica's white one was gone. The bitch was probably somewhere spreading her legs for that nigga. No matter. Her ass was grass. He got out and walked into the house.

"Fucking whore!" he yelled as he saw the broken dishes. He rushed into the dining room.

The moment he saw the overturned china cabinet, he knew. *Sneaky, conniving slut!* The empty hole confirmed it. He whipped out his phone and dialed.

"Ace, everybody ready? Good. Send Slick and the two boys now. If that bitch Jessica is there, tell them to hold her for me. She's got something that belongs to me. I'm on my way."

He stomped out, slamming the door behind him. In his vehicle, he dialed another number. "Farrelli? It's Bullet. Yeah, I know. It ain't over yet. Yeah. Yeah. Listen, I got to finish it. I didn't start it. Cover me and you get a million. First thing tomorrow. Put it on the Ricans fighting over turf. You know how. An' the mil's only a down payment. Right. Later."

Bullet stood in the front room of his dope house on Nixon. Ace, Trey, Brew, Conch, and H-Bomb were with him.

"I sent Slick, Nate, and Pee-Wee to Sugar's. I told them what you said about the hoes. And Jessica. They'll try not to kill the nigga."

"Okay, Ace. Now everybody strap up except H-Bomb. The house is closed until we get back. Nobody in, nobody gets served. Don't worry about the law. I got it fixed. We going to Gulfport to knock that Rican, Jesse. Then it's all ours."

Brew said, "What about Cisco?"

"He's dead. Like I said, kill Jesse, an' we got it all."

The men got busy. Two scoped AR15s and two shotguns, along with a Calico, two Uzis, and their personal pistols went into the Suburban. Ace had a bad feeling about this, but he was down with Bullet, so he kept quiet.

Things had changed since the last time they had tangled with Jesse. Ace alone knew that it was Cisco's intervention that kept the dude from bringing it to them. He could only hope that they could surprise him, do him, then get clear of Gulfport. Their only other option was to get all their men off the street and fight a real war. Even then, the outcome would be in doubt.

When they got to Highway 49, Bullet told them the plan. "Club Loco is where he hangs out these days. There's a back stairway leading up to his office. Usually he's up there with his girl an' maybe a couple of his boys. There is always one guy at the bottom to keep anybody from coming up unannounced.

"Ace, we're gonna park out front. Go around back on foot and do the guard. Thirty seconds after you go to the back, we'll pull up and all rush the stairs. Everybody inside dies. Then we catch Old Pass Road back to Biloxi. I don't have grease with the Gulfport aws, so we gotta be quick. Got it?"

The plan seemed kind of risky to Ace, but he didn't have a better one. Best to do this and get it over with. His Glock 9 mm was the only silenced weapon they'd brought. Conch and Trey took the ARs. Between them they had a couple hundred rounds before re-loading. Brew took one of the new Uzis and would bring a second one for Ace. Bullet had the Cobra.

Ace peeped around the corner of the building. Pulling his head back, he thought, *At least he was right about this part.* A lone Hispanic dude was sitting at the base of a set of stairs, smoking a joint. Stuffing the silenced Glock down the front of his pants, Ace stepped around the building.

"Hey! What you doin' back here?"

"Takin' a piss," Ace replied, as he unzipped his pants.

The roar of the Suburban's engine as it came around the other side of the building distracted the guard. Not Ace, since he expected it. When the man turned in surprise, Ace pulled the pistol and shot him twice in the back.

The man fell as the truck emptied of Bullet and his men. "Let's do this," Bullet said, motioning for Conch to lead the way up the stairs.

The steps vibrated as the men rushed upward. Conch didn't hesitate. He threw open the door at the top, stepping into the room. Four men sat at a table, playing dominoes. Two were Black, and the other two, Hispanic. As they looked up in surprise, Conch opened fire with the assault rifle. All four men were down by the time Brew and Trey joined him.

The room stank of blood, shit, and cordite. Bullet crowded in and pointed to a closed door. "In there!" He cut loose with two rounds from his shotgun, and the door flew open. When they entered, all they saw was an empty bed with tangled sheets. The smell of marijuana was strong in the air. The heavy thump of a rap beat could be heard through the walls.

Jesse Verdun's latest freak had been riding his pole when he heard the first shots. Her hot, tight pussy pulling at his dick and the way her soft ass felt against his thighs almost cost him his life right then.

Throwing her off him, he jumped up and dragged her through the door leading to the club. Dick swinging, he leapt down the stairs and into the space behind the bar. Yelling in Spanish and English to his men, he dug beneath the bar for his nine.

"Through there," Bullet yelled to his men.

Ace, clutching the Uzi he'd retrieved from Brew, was the first to comply. As he stepped onto the landing, the door at the bottom swung open and three men burst through. He spread his legs and turned the Uzi loose. The spray of bullets tore into the mass of flesh at the stairs' bottom.

The men lay dead at the bottom, and Ace turned his head to tell Bullet it was clear. That cost him. Jesse, still naked as the day he was born, stepped into the well and shot Ace three times.

Bullet blasted with the shotgun. The first shot missed Jesse, who'd ducked back into the barroom. Bullet's second blast of .00 buckshot fired through the door and wall, caught Jesse in the chest and groin. Bullet was already hollering for Brew and Trey to take Ace to the truck.

As they barreled onto Pass Road heading east, Bullet, from the passenger seat, turned to look into the rear. Trey shook his head. Ace was dead. Bullet sat back with a sigh. He and Ace had been together through it all. Ace was the voice of reason that kept him from self-destructing.

His anger built as they drove on. Sugar and them bitches would pay. He also felt a sense of satisfaction. Jesse was dead. He knew he'd hit him. Nothing could stop him now. He would have it all.

CHAPTER TWENTY-FIVE

As they sped away from Gulfport, with Ace's body in the rear, Bullet and his crew were charged with emotion. They had done it! And they were still alive. Except for Ace.

Trey and Brew's mood quickly turned somber. Both men knew that tonight's action would set off a chain of events that would have far-reaching consequences. Trey thought about the early days when Bullet was a rising star in the cocaine underworld.

"What we gonna do with Ace?" Trey knew that Ace and Bullet were tight. He also knew that there wouldn't be time to mourn him properly. Not if they were to survive.

"Drop me off at Nixon. I'll tell you what to do then."

Bullet's tone didn't allow for argument. Brew took a left, and they jumped on the 110. In fifteen minutes, the vehicle pulled into the driveway of the crack house. Bullet sat for a minute in silence.

"Get on Ten and head toward Pass Christian. Take the Long Beach exit. Stay on the feeder and take the first road to the right. When it dead-ends, there will be a pit about a hundred yards past the fence. Weigh him down and put him there."

"But—" Trey began.

Bullet's voice rose in volume. "You think I like the idea of dumping him like a load of garbage? If I could, I'd send him off like a hero. Right now, we got to finish this shit."

Trey nodded his head and Bullet got out. Leaving Conch in the back seat, Trey replaced his boss in the front passenger seat. The men took off.

"Hey, Trey, that was some gangster shit back in Gulfport. We showed them motherfuckers what real niggas all about, huh?" Conch said.

"Kid, you got shit for brains." Brew glared at him through the rearview mirror for a moment. "All we did was open up a can of worms. Could be we started a full-scale war. Don' you know what happens in a war? Soldiers die, boy. Like Ace back there."

"I ain't scared to die. I'm gonna go out like a real G—just the way Ace did."

"That's why he called you shit-for-brains, youngster. The dope game is what it is. We ain't in it to be famous. We in it to get paid. We do what we gotta do to stack our paper. You can't stack money in hell." Trey sat back and closed his eyes.

"What you think about all this shit with Bullet and his girl?"

"I'll tell you, Brew. I ain't real crazy about it. Me, I catch my bitch fuckin' up, I just kick her ass out and move on to the next one. Can't blame the nigga for layin' a little pipe if the ho givin' it up," Trey said.

"I don' know, man. I kinda feel where Bullet comin' from. I catch a nigga up in mines, I'm-a cap his ass and hers too. Him for disrespectin' me and her for being a no-good ho," Brew said.

Conch spoke up from the rear. "That's why I ain't got no girl. I just fuck whoever I want and don't worry about who she with when I'm not up in it."

"An' that's why your dick's gonna rot off one of these days, pushin' up in these dope fiends. That's our exit comin' up, Brew," Trey reminded.

Brew followed Bullet's directions, and soon they were at the barricade marking the end of the last road.

"Shit, is this the place? Some kind of dump?" asked Conch.

"Naw. The reason it took so long to finish this section of Ten is that some group filed a suit to protect some birds. Sandhill Cranes, I think. This is where they had started to build about ten years ago and had to stop. Let's do this. Brew, we got any rope in here?"

"I don't think so, but there's a couple of old chains back there with Ace."

The body was just starting to stiffen, but the three men steeled themselves and, ignoring the blood and bullet wounds, they manhandled Ace across the barricade and over the mounds to the water-filled pit.

There, they wrapped chunks of asphalt in the chains and bound them to the body. Standing on a stone shelf, Trey and Brew managed to throw the heavy load a few feet out into the water. The body, after a big splash, sank quickly.

"Old Ace was for real. He was player all the way." Trey's words reflected all their thoughts.

"I guess you got his old job now. Tryin' to keep Bullet from goin' psycho on everybody ain't gonna be easy," Brew said.

"You know it's gonna take all of us to keep that maniac in check. But he's the boss. An' he's right. We got to finish this. Let's get on back and see what's up," Trey said.

The three men turned and left Ace to the fish.

CHAPTER TWENTY-SIX

Bullet sat on the sofa in his crack house and took a long gulp from his second glass of cognac. He shed no tears, but that didn't mean he didn't feel grief. He and Ace went way back. They'd come up together. He let himself remember.

Fifteen years ago, Bullet was thirteen years old. He was born in Moss Point, and up until just before his thirteenth birthday, he had been the typical bad-ass little boy growing up in a small town. Bullet had always had a temper.

His daddy's work was sporadic. Sometimes he'd catch on for a couple of months when one of the civilian contractors at the shipyard needed extra help. Other times he worked the shrimp boats as labor.

His mother had a weak heart. She did housework for some of the wealthy in Pascagoula when her health permitted. Which was seldom. Mostly she just stayed home with Bullet and his three sisters. They were poor.

That was probably the biggest source of his rage. Kids

being kids, he was teased at school about his clothes and beat-up shoes. He responded by fighting. Any and everybody. Sometimes he got his ass kicked, but not often.

At first, his old man kicked his butt every time he got thrown out of school, but soon enough he just raised hell and let it go. His mama kept sending him back. She was the only person in the world who could reason with him.

His father's sister lived in Biloxi, in the heart of the Black neighborhood, just off Division and Main. Three days before his birthday, Bullet's mama convinced his father to take them to a church concert in Pensacola, Florida, about an hour's drive away.

Bullet begged to stay at his aunt's house in Biloxi while his parents and three sisters attended the concert. His parents were supposed to come get him on the way home. They never did.

A truck on Highway 90 between Moss Point and Mobile lost a load of pulpwood. The huge logs tumbled from the broken stays on the truck directly onto the old Caravan carrying Bullet's mother and father, along with his three sisters. None of them survived.

His aunt was an alcoholic with a steady procession of boyfriends. After the funerals, Bullet begged her to let him live with her. His only other option was state-sponsored foster care. When she learned she would receive the small life insurance policy in effect on Bullet's father, as well as a Social Security check, she took him in.

Whatever small moral guidance he'd received up to that point vanished. He never set foot in church after that, and never had any real supervision. As long as the checks kept coming, his aunt didn't care what he did.

Bullet had met Ace on previous trips to his aunt's; their house was three doors down on the same street. Ace was a little taller than Bullet, but slimmer. Bullet

liked hanging around with him because he was quiet. He
didn't run his mouth a lot, but he was smart. And from
the beginning, he followed Bullet's lead.

Ace's Uncle Pete was a crack dealer. He worked the
same block that their main rock house would later be sit-
uated on. The two boys started hanging out with Pete
after school. They would run errands for him, to the gro-
cery store, KFC, carrying messages to his workers, etc.

Pete would pay them and send them on their way. Ace
was kin, and Nixon Street was no place for his nephew to
be hanging out. Things changed when Bullet's family
died.

"Man, I'm tired of being broke and poor. I wanna be
like Pete. See that 'Vette he drives? His pockets always
fat, and he don't chase pussy. Pussy chases him."

"Yeah, Unc got it goin' on. But he ain't gonna hook us
up. We can't go out there on our own, we'd get fucked-
up."

The two boys sat on the back porch of Ace's parents'
house. They had snuck a forty-ounce bottle of beer from
the refrigerator and were sharing it.

"I'll bet he would help us out if we talked to him. He
could find something for us to do. One day we gon' own
this town, man."

Ace looked over and nodded. When the boys got to
Pete's house on Nixon, they heard a big commotion from
the back room. When they went back, they could make
out what Pete was saying.

"I tole you, boy. I don't take no shorts on my money!
When I say fifteen hundred, I don't mean fourteen. This
the second time. I got to teach you a lesson 'bout fuckin'
around!"

Standing in the doorway, Bullet could see two of Pete's
workers holding a third man between them. The eyes of

the man in the middle were wide with fear. Pete's jaws were tight with anger, and he was pulling on a pair of leather gloves. Pete's big .357 was stuck in the small of the man's back.

"Uncle Pete. Let us take care of this for you. We need jobs anyway."

Pete whirled. His nephew and his friend Bullet stood just outside the doorway. His first impulse was to run them off. They didn't need to see this. Then he saw the determined looks on their faces.

These boys are what? Thirteen? Fourteen? he thought. *And damn! They're getting big.* He made his decision.

He addressed Ace, but instinctively he looked at Bullet. "This nigga owes me money. This ain't the first time he fucked me over. How would you handle this, nephew?"

Bullet carried a baseball bat in his belt. One of those little eighteen-inch souvenir Louisville sluggers. He pulled it out as he walked into the room. It was already whipping forward as he stepped past Pete.

CRACK!

The wood exploded against the man's knee.

He screamed in pain and sagged.

CRACK!

Bullet capped the other knee.

Ace stepped forward and put a hand on his shoulder. "Enough."

Both boys looked up at Pete, ignoring the whimpering man on the floor. Pete's shock was evident. So was his satisfaction.

"Take this nigga to Biloxi Regional and dump him by the emergency room. He knows better than to say how he got hurt."

The men left, supporting the whimpering worker.

"Come here, boys." Pete withdrew a wad of cash.

"This is the take off his corner. Take it and buy you some clothes. Come see me tomorrow night at six. You two can have his job."

"Thanks, Unc. How much to buy us two guns? We don't want nobody to get ideas about our age."

Pete looked at Ace with new respect. These two would bear watching. He smiled and led them to the attic, where his weapons were stored.

That was the true beginning of a long partnership. It was Bullet's penchant for violence that got them in. They were never broke or poor again. Just as Ace predicted, they had to prove themselves. The first customer to try and take advantage of their age and size got introduced to the Louisville Slugger, and the second got his car shot up. That pretty much did it.

Bullet and Ace were never short with their drop, and Pete took note. By the time they were sixteen, the boys had four spots to take care of. They had bought a Navigator, had gold grills, Rolexes, and diamond pendants.

Bullet had become the most feared man in the hood. If you crossed him, blood flowed. Ace was the only calming influence he knew. Unofficially, despite their age, they were second only to Pete in his organization.

They were seventeen when Pete got busted. His connection was in Mobile, and he was there when the DEA made a raid. Ace was able to clear the dope he had on hand and the money out of his house.

Bullet wasted no time. Within a week, he made contact with a Puerto Rican named Francisco De Leon. Cisco became his new supplier. Now Bullet and Ace had their own organization.

The rest was history. Between Bullet's ruthlessness and Ace's instincts, their rise was quick. When their economics said they could expand, Bullet either absorbed or killed his rivals. He didn't really care which.

And now, just when they were in a position to have it all, Ace was dead.

Bullet rose from the sofa and began to pace. He'd have to work with what he had left. Trey, Brew, Conch, and the rest weren't Ace, but they were loyal. And he still had an ace in the hole. Farelli.

CHAPTER TWENTY-SEVEN

Captain Farelli sat and stared out at the chaos that was the Homicide squad room. He had just answered his second call from Bullet. This was rapidly turning into a real cluster fuck. One million dollars was a powerful incentive, especially since it would add enough cash to his special "retirement fund" for him to maybe walk away.

Farelli had been in the Biloxi Police Department for twenty-five years. He had seen Sugar and Cole run the mean streets of The Strip as kids. He had chased Bullet and Ace through backyards and around corners all over town. And he had finally wised up.

Not being a native of the city, he had taken with a grain of salt the stories of the massive corruption in the city government. After all, South Boston, where Farelli grew up, had its share of crooked cops and city officials. This place was different, though. Sin City, Southern style.

Like most things in the South, Biloxi was not at all like its appearance. Underneath the laid-back, slow-motion exterior ran a ruthless, larcenous energy. The city had long been a haven for the criminal element. Prostitution, gambling, drugs, and smuggling permeated its social structure, and had done so for decades. Of course, these activities bred wholesale governmental corruption.

Farelli had worked clean for more than five years before he gave in. Watching his fellow officers and city officials get rich on kickbacks and openly living lavish lifestyles finally became too much. When he made sergeant, he started to accept the envelopes he had previously refused.

He had never been stupid, though, nor too greedy. The Feds had successfully investigated and prosecuted more than one city official who had gotten too comfortable and overt with his activities. The so-called "Dixie Mafia," who controlled most of the vice, had been the target of three investigations in recent history.

Rumor was that the Justice Department was about to undertake a fourth. Farelli did not want to get caught in the crunch. He had saved up a nice nest egg. This payment from Bullet would just about allow him to take early retirement and never have to work again.

Putting the murders of Francisco De Leon and his girl-friend on a drug turf war between Gulfport and Biloxi wouldn't be too difficult. Now Bullet claimed he had to finish a situation between him and Sugar. Farelli knew that any move against Sugar would eventually involve John Coleman. And Cole was bad news. Farelli was pulled from his contemplations by the shrill sound of the phone.

"Farelli. What? Okay. I'm on my way. Just secure the scene and wait for me."

He hit the door on the run, barking commands into his handheld radio. Fuck! That motherfucking Bullet was going to get all their asses in a sling! His men had just tried to kill Sugar at his house. They got iced instead. Two more bodies.

As he waited for his driver to pull up in front of Police

Headquarters, his thoughts were racing. That fucking psycho was out of control. Farelli had no idea that Bullet intended to litter the whole coast with dead bodies in a twenty-four-hour period. Farelli knew Bullet was a mean, brutal killer, and that he had iron control over his crew.

But Sugar and Cole? Those two hadn't been a problem for him in years. Cole had left years ago, and Sugar had a legitimate business. Farelli remembered the times he had gone to The Strip to clean up their messes. They had always been ready to settle differences with violence. No matter what the odds.

They were smart. This once, Bullet might have bitten off more than he could chew. Farelli smiled. Wouldn't it be wonderful if he collected the mil' from Bullet tomorrow, and then Sugar or Cole whacked him? Then he'd really be off the hook. He was still smiling as he slid into the passenger seat of his unmarked. Time to take out some insurance.

Pee-Wee huddled behind the truck parked in front of Sugar's garage. His body trembled in fear. Nate and Slick were dead. He'd watched the heavy slugs tear them apart. Blood and pieces of Nate's skull and brain were everywhere.

He took a couple of deep breaths. *Shit. Bullet is gonna be pissed! Fuck him!* Ace never told them that this nigga was some kind of fuckin' commando or soldier or somethin'. They might have done it different. Pee-Wee knew that the only reason he wasn't dead like his two friends was that the dude didn't see him.

Who was this nigga? Shit, he sold barbecue, for Christ's sake. All Pee-Wee wanted right now was to get as far away from Sugar as possible. And it needed to be pretty quick. Before Sugar decided to check his yard.

Pee-Wee cautiously stuck his head out and peeked

around the vehicle. Sugar was just going back into the house. For an instant, the thought crossed Pee-Wee's mind that now would be a good time to try and take him. He rejected that idea.

Plan B sounded a lot better. Get the fuck back to the dope house and let Bullet and Ace decide how they were going to deal with this dude. With any luck they'd pick somebody else to do the dirty work. He'd much rather sling dope.

Their car was parked back near the entrance to the drive. The choice was made for Pee-Wee when he heard the faint, distant sound of sirens. Cops! Being careful to keep Sugar's truck between himself and the open front door, Pee-Wee ran in a crouch back toward the street.

CHAPTER TWENTY-EIGHT

Sugar sat on his front porch and waited for the police. For a day that had started with so much promise, this one had sure turned to shit. Jessica's warning had saved his life. His mind churned. They were all in the shit. Again.

Alana was dead. The memory of the fantastic sex they'd had just hours ago ate at him. Their good-bye fuck had been just that. A permanent good-bye. He shook himself mentally. If that psycho asshole of Jessica's had anything to say about it, him, Jessica, and even Nora would soon join Alana.

The bullhorn roared. "You! Take two steps forward and lie face down. Keep your hands away from your body!"

Sugar complied.

He felt a heavy weight on his back and allowed his arms to be wrenched behind his back and cuffed.

The questions came like gunshots.

"Is anybody in the house?"

"Are they armed?"

"What happened?"

They quieted when he started to speak, rapidly, but clearly. "My name is Jameel White. It is my house. Some men tried to break in and kill us. I shot them with my shotgun. My girlfriend is locked in her room. She's the one that called you. The shotgun is on the wall beside the door. They are dead."

"What's your woman's name?"

"Elnora."

"Elnora. This is the police. Everything is all right. Come outside now, ma'am. Please."

They all waited in tense silence for a minute. By twisting his head, Sugar could see Nora timidly fill the doorway.

"Nora, baby. It's all right. Don't be scared. Come on out."

Her eyes swept the yard trying to locate his voice. When she saw him on the ground in handcuffs, it seemed to galvanize her into action. She charged the group.

"What the fuck are you doing? Let him go! He saved our lives. He didn't do anything wrong. Let him go!"

The short, drab-looking woman took the cops aback. The one with the bullhorn tried to calm her down.

"It's okay, ma'am. We didn't hurt him. It's just procedure."

"Procedure, my ass. Let him go! Sugar!"

Sugar was shocked. He had, in all the time he'd known her, never heard her curse or even raise her voice. The cops huddled up for a moment. Several officers were still on high alert, guns pointed toward the lit doorway.

"Okay, ma'am. We're going to take the cuffs off him. Both of you will be placed in a police car. We have to check out the house and wait for our captain to get here. Please, calm down."

Nora didn't say anything as they uncuffed Sugar and escorted them both to a police car. When they put Sugar in the rear of one, and started to lead her away, she struggled. The one obviously in charge waved them off, and they let her stay with him.

She immediately slid over next to Sugar and he wrapped her in his arms. For the next hour and a half, the place was a beehive. Crime scene personnel, the coroner, and several detectives showed up. After what seemed like forever, a man in a suit came over to their car. He opened the rear door and leaned against the roof of the car.

"Mr. White, Miss Sharp, my name is Captain Farrelli. We have checked you both out, and the crime scene techs say this all could have happened the way you say. We've got to wait until the techs finish and a representative from the DA gets here, but I don't think there'll be any charges.

"We've had a double murder in North Biloxi, a gang shootout in Gulfport, and now this. I don't think they're related, but you never know. You don't know a drug dealer named Ollie Marsh, do you?"

Nora opened her mouth to answer, but Sugar squeezed her shoulder. He knew that their caller ID and cell phones showed calls from Jessica and Alana, among others. He looked into Farrelli's eyes as he spoke.

"Captain, Ollie Marsh is the boyfriend of a friend of ours. Somehow, he got the impression I'm sleeping with her. I haven't seen him, and I have nothing to do with his business. I don't want any trouble with him or anyone else, but I won't let anybody hurt Nora or me."

Farrelli was silent for a minute. Now it was his turn to gaze into Sugar's eyes.

"I can't argue with that. Years ago, when I was a patrol

sergeant, I had a few dealing with a couple of youngsters on The Strip. Didn't you used to hang with John Coleman?"

"Yeah. But I don't get in trouble anymore. I've got a business. I haven't seen Cole in years."

"Right. If I remember correctly, Coleman didn't like anybody messing with his friends. If you do see or hear from him, tell him we're not looking for him. As long as he stays out of trouble and off my radar, we got no problems. You two might need to find somewhere to spend the night."

"Thank you, Captain. I'll deliver your message. We'll be all right. We can handle ourselves."

"Yeah. You do that."

When Farelli was gone, Nora asked, "What was he talking about? What's Cole got to do with this?"

"Jess told me that Farrelli is on Bullet's payroll. Farelli knows that Bullet killed Cisco and Alana. He knows he tried to kill me. He can't go against him without putting himself at risk. But he knows Cole. He figures that Cole can take care of Bullet and will do it for me and Jessica. If he does, then Farelli is off the hook. He wants me to sic Cole on Bullet. If I do, then Cole or me won't get into trouble if we're careful."

"He gave you guys permission to kill Bullet?"

"That's about what it amounts to. Biloxi is corrupt as hell, but sometimes it works to our advantage."

After the DA told them to hang around until the inquest, Sugar and Nora loaded his truck and left the house. He hoped they would see it again.

CHAPTER TWENTY-NINE

Trey opened the door to the crack house on Nixon and let himself and Brew in. Conch hung outside while Trey and Brew went inside to discuss what had just gone down. The three men had just finished the unpleasant task of disposing of Ace's body. They, like the other members of Bullet's crew, were sobered by the thought that either of them could have been dead along with, or instead of, Ace.

Both were hard young men. They had been hustling dope up and down the Gulf Coast since their teens, along with Ace and Bullet. Without question, Bullet had always been their leader, and they had come a long way following him. But Ace had always been the brain.

He was the one who tempered Bullet's violent and homicidal personality. Who would do it now? No answers had come during the grisly job, but both had decided that they would stay down with, and loyal to Bullet until the end. Both also hoped they would survive the shit storm that had been initiated last night.

Bullet was waiting for them in the front room. "We need to talk."

His face was haggard, and Trey and Brew knew that the death of Ace had hit him hard. Bullet quickly recounted the series of events that had led him to Cisco's house.

"So you see, when he told me about having to be served by that punk Jesse, I had to do something. You know he hates us an' would fuck us over the minute Cisco was gone. I didn't want to dust Cisco, but he went crazy when I tole him about his bitch fucking that nigga Sugar.

"That ho Jessica was in on it too. The Rican bitch must've tole her I was comin' 'cause she split with all my stash. I thought the ho was dead. I paid Farelli a whole mil' to let us regroup. We only got one day. I'm tellin' y'all this so you know: You two are gonna help me finish this.

"We gotta press the docks in North Biloxi. Cisco's people don' know who's behind him and Jesse getting killed. We're gonna give them a way to keep movin' product until they can find a new boss. We'll do Gulfport too. I know we can sell the idea to 'em 'cause they need us right now.

"At the same time, we gotta find Sugar and that bitch Jessica. Pee-Wee got back a while ago. It looks like the nigga got Slick and Nate. Pee-Wee got out just before the laws got there. Brew, you wait till later today, then find them. Bust a cap in Sugar's ass, but if you can, bring the bitch to me. My money too.

"Trey, you an' me gonna work the docks till we get with the Ricans. Bring two more boys an' we'll take your car. Have Conch an' H-Bomb run the house."

Bullet led the men out and down the street to the car. Ace's death had fucked his plans up, but he knew it was all a part of life. He was confident now that he could still come out of this on top of it all. And he would. He could feel it.

CHAPTER THIRTY

Jessica sat limply on the sofa. Mary and her husband had just left. It was a couple of hours past dawn, and they had spent most of the night ferrying furniture from Mary's house to the warehouse.

The place had been a wreck, abandoned, apparently, since they had all lived there years ago. The three of them had cleaned out the living area and brought enough of Mary's stuff to make it livable. Mary's family wouldn't be needing it for a while anyway.

After slipping away from the condo just before Bullet arrived, she'd gone straight to Mary. Following Sugar's instructions, she had awoken her friend and told her what had happened. It took a while to convince Mary, then her husband, that it just wouldn't be safe for them to stay.

The thirty grand she produced from Bullet's bag helped. They had moved enough stuff in two trips to make the place a suitable hideout for a few days. Mary and her husband were en route to Jackson with their kids. John would rent them a cottage at a place he knew just off the Natchez Trace, and they would stay until Sugar called them home.

Jessica knew that Bullet would try Mary's as well as Sugar's home in an effort to find her. When thoughts of Alana began to intrude on her consciousness, she roused herself. Dumping Bullet's leather bag onto the floor, she began to sort and count the money. There was $230,000 left.

Taking the money had been a last-minute inspiration. She knew that it would fuck with Bullet's head. The cash was the least of it. She knew she couldn't fight Bullet like a man and expect to win. That was for Sugar and Cole. But for all the years of putting up with his indifferent ways, his abuse, and most of all for Alana, she could extract her own revenge. All she needed was an internet connection, and Sugar's account number in Belize.

She was fleshing out her plans when she heard a noise downstairs. It was the roll-up doors opening. When Sugar killed the engine to his truck, she was already racing down the stairs.

"Sugar! Oh man! Alana!"

Jessica wept as he wrapped her in his arms. The tears she had forced down inside her, along with her grief, all came pouring out. Sugar held her a long time. Unnoticed by them, Nora made several trips between the truck and the upstairs living area. When Jessica's tears stopped, Sugar led her up the steps.

While Nora bustled from room to room, Sugar brought Jessica up-to-date on all that had happened since her frantic call to him. He finished with the description of how Captain Farelli had let them get clothes and personal items out of the house after the bodies were removed. He'd even brought his strongbox and three pistols.

Jessica told him Cole was on his way, and Sugar breathed a sigh of relief. Now he'd be able to fight back.

After about thirty minutes of hard work, he managed to clear the rusty pipes of dirty brown water and even light the ancient hot water heater. He took a shower and collapsed on the bed in his old room.

Jessica had just finished stuffing the cash back into the bag when she heard a sound behind her. She had planned to take a shower, run Elnora out of Sugar's room, and join him in bed. She had enough cash to set a Game record when she dumped a whole two hundred grand on him after he fucked her down.

"Jessica?"

She turned to see Nora standing behind her. "Hi, I was just about to come looking for you."

"Can I talk to you for a while?"

"Sure," Jessica answered. She thought Nora looked kind of different. She couldn't exactly put her finger on how.

Gracefully, Elnora sank into a cross-legged sitting position opposite her.

"Did Sugar ever tell you how we met? How he saved my life?"

Jessica noticed the effort this was causing her. Nora was tense, tiny beads of sweat dotting her forehead. Curiosity arose immediately. Jessica had always wanted to know Nora's history. Sugar wouldn't talk about it, and forbade any of them questioning Nora.

"No. What happened?"

Heaving a deep sigh, Nora began her story.

"I was seventeen. My boyfriend, Abu, used to buy big sacks of weed from the docks in North Biloxi—you know how the shrimp boats sell their loads over there—and I was with him when he went that day. The guy he bought it from wasn't there, and we had to wait. After about an hour, this young kid told us he had unloaded his boat and was waiting for us in a warehouse down the dock.

"Abu got his gun, and, not wanting to leave me in the car, told me to come with him. When we got inside the place was dark. Abu shouted for the boat captain, and a voice from the other side of the building yelled, 'Over here.' We hadn't taken two steps before they jumped us.

"Something hit me in the face, and I heard a loud noise, a gunshot, as I screamed and fell. They dragged me across the concrete floor to the middle of the room. I never saw Abu again. There were four of them. One beat me with his fist while the other hacked at my blouse and jeans with a knife. That's how my breast got cut.

"They raped me. Over and over. Everywhere, beating me all the time." Nora's breath was getting ragged and her body trembled violently as she relived the horrible experience.

Jessica went cold. It was hard enough imagining the terror and pain Elnora had gone through, but she remembered the bloody, tattered bundle Sugar had brought home. She shuddered. "Go on, baby," she whispered softly.

Taking a deep breath, Nora continued. "I don't know how long it went on. My mind just broke. Went away. It was almost like they were doing these terrible things to someone else. I knew I was going to die. I wanted to. I just wanted it to be over."

"Then Sugar was there. There was a *crack*, and the guy on top of me stiffened. His eyes got wide, and he collapsed. The shooting started. I couldn't see what was happening. The noise stopped, and the man on top of me was gone. There was another guy leaning over me, and I recoiled in fear.

"'Sssh. Sssh. It's all right. They're all dead. They won't ever hurt you again. I'll take care of you. My name is Sugar.' I'll never forget that moment. He covered me with his own shirt, and I could see that he was bleeding.

"He picked me up like a baby. 'Abu?' I said. 'I'm sorry. Your friend's gone.'

"The next thing I remember is waking up here. Sugar washing me. You and the girls. I was so afraid. The only thing I knew is that if I stayed close to Sugar, nobody could hurt me again. I refused to go home. I made him tell my momma I ran away with a boy.

"I've never talked about this with anyone. Not even Sugar. Why am I telling you this now? It's simple. I'm healing up inside. In my head. Everybody treats me like I'm not even there, and I know that's my fault. I just couldn't handle life, or people.

"But I've been better for a while now. What I'm trying to say, Jessica, is that The Game is over. It's no good for Sugar, and it's no good for you and the other girls."

Elnora squared her shoulders and looked Jessica in the eyes. "And from now on, Sugar is mine."

CHAPTER THIRTY-ONE

Cole sat in his Caddy at the corner of Camellia Street and Southern Avenue. His mind was awash with memories. It had been years since he had seen The Strip. The broad street was filled with clubs, massage parlors, titty bars, and whores. This was home. The whole topography was different, yet the same.

Jessica had given him directions to the warehouse where they were holed up. He'd see his old childhood friends soon. First, though, he'd gather some information on his own. Sugar was a tough dude, and could handle himself, but the kind of shit he was involved in now was Cole's bread and butter.

An old friend, T-Mike, had given the lowdown on the new setup here. Cole had stopped in Pass Christian and caught T-Mike at his mom's home. The young rapper still worked the clubs while he was trying to break out, and directed Cole to the strip joint he was looking for.

Parking the car, Cole checked his weapons. After going in, he stood in the entrance to let his eyes adjust. Even this early in the afternoon, there were quite a few customers. Strippers performed on each of three small stages. In the darker recesses of the room he could see women in thongs pushing their asses and tits up on dudes, who sat mesmerized.

She wasn't among these girls either. Eyes roving, Cole threaded his way through tables where near-naked wait-resses served watered-down, overpriced drinks. At the bar, he caught the bartender's eye.

"I'm looking for Taneesha."

"She'll be on about twenty minutes. Have a seat either here or at a table."

"I need to see her now. I'm an old friend from out of town. Where's her dressing room?"

Before he answered, the man's eyes flicked to the left, which told Cole what he wanted to know.

"Give me your name and I'll send back a message. Hump doesn't allow personal visits until after the dance shift."

"No problem." Cole strolled off to his right, the direc-tion he was sure the dressing rooms were in.

The bartender shouted, "Hey," but didn't move.

As Cole expected, the door toward which he was headed opened, and a bouncer stepped through. The man looked like an NFL lineman. Well over six feet and wide. His voice was surprisingly soft, considering the mean mug he was displaying.

"Yo, brother, you can't come back there. Have a seat or I'll have to show you out."

Cole didn't slow. He let his "cooler" drop into his hand from the sleeve of his leather jacket. It was just an old-fashioned sap, like Reuben taught them to make when they were kids. A twelve-inch bolt, surrounded com-pletely with flat washers, and the whole thing wrapped tightly with electrical tape. A bone breaker.

Cole slapped the bouncer on the head almost gently,

(he didn't want to kill him) then harder on the right knee. The man crashed to the floor, semi-conscious. Cole knew that even when his head cleared, the leg wouldn't support him.

He stepped around the fallen man and through the door, closing it behind him. Dropping the sap into his pocket, he pulled his Glock. The first door on his left was the one he wanted. He flung it open and entered with his pistol.

"Hello, Hump," he said to the balding White man behind the desk.

"Oh, shit! Johnny! What the fuck do you think you're doing? Where the hell is Slade?"

"He got sleepy. They told me I couldn't come back here."

The whole Biloxi Strip was owned by the so-called "Dixie Mafia." Hump worked for them. Times had changed, though, and Hump knew Cole from the time he was a hell-raising whore's kid here. That meant he knew not to fuck with him.

"Okay, kid. What do you want?"

Hump was sweating. He hoped Cole hadn't come to make good on Sugar's threats of what would happen if he mistreated Taneesha.

"I need to talk to Taneesha. Family business. That okay with you?"

The relief was evident on Hump's face. "No problem. I can get one of the others to cover her shift." He picked up the phone. "Tell Taneesha to come to my office. Now."

Cole heard a door open down the hall. He stepped to the side, pistol ready just in case. Hump was talking to the bartender on the intercom, reassuring him.

Taneesha charged into the office wearing only what looked like a couple of leather straps and a dog collar. She marched up to Hump's desk. "What?"

Noticing the direction of his look, she turned. The first thing she noticed was the gun. She backed up into the desk. Then she recognized him.

"Cole!" she squealed.

When she threw herself into his arms, he barely avoided poking her with the pistol. With his free hand, he grabbed a handful of her soft ass and pulled her to him.

"What's up, baby? Long time, huh?"

"Where you been? How long you stayin'? You seen Sugar, Jess, and Lana yet? You know I don't see the girls as much as I should, but I do keep up with Sugar and Nora . . ."

Cole grew still. His smile vanished. "Alana's dead. Come on. We need to talk. Get dressed. You're coming with me."

Ignoring the shock on her face, he pushed her back out into the hall.

Chapter Thirty-Two

Cole turned to Hump. "I've got my car out front. A black Cadillac with Texas plates. I'm gonna park it in the back lot and take Taneesha's car for a while. Don't let nobody fuck with it."

Hump didn't know what was going on, but he'd heard Cole tell Taneesha that the fine-ass Puerto Rican chick they used to run with was dead. He knew how close Sugar's little group had been and he knew there would soon be dead bodies in Biloxi. He was just glad it didn't have anything to do with him or his business.

"Sure, Johnny. You need anything?"

"Naw. Just watch my ride."

He met Taneesha in the hall, tying the belt to a long coat.

"Where's your car?"

"Out back. A maroon Acura."

"Meet me there." He turned away before she could respond.

When he parked next to her, he locked up and slid into the Acura's passenger seat.

"Where to?" she asked.

"Someplace close, where we can talk."

"Then we don't need to drive. Come on."

They got out, she locked up the car, then pointed toward the back of the lot. "The Ocean Way is still open."

As they crossed the parking lot en route to the old motel on the next street, Cole told her what he knew about Alana's death and Sugar's trouble. He watched the shock, grief, and anger cross her face.

"Why the hell didn't Jessica or Sugar call me?"

"They didn't have time, and knowing Sugar, he didn't want you in the middle of it."

"Fuck that! I really don't know that nigga Bullet, but he's bad news. I tried to tell Jessica that."

When they entered the motel parking lot, Taneesha went to the window and came back with a key. The room was on the back side of the motel. As they walked around the building, Taneesha asked, "What do you want me to do?"

"I need information. I haven't been here in a long time. Who works for Bullet? Where do they sling their shit?"

Taneesha opened the door to the room. "Okay, I can help with that."

Cole nodded and went straight for the phone next to the bed. "All right. Give me a minute to check on Sugar and the girls."

Taneesha sat on the bed next to him while he dialed and confirmed that Sugar, Jessica, and Nora were hanging tight at the warehouse. As Cole hung up the phone, Taneesha stood in front of him.

"Okay, now I need you to help me," she said.

The puzzled look left Cole's face when she turned and undid the buckle under her coat. She hadn't dressed, just covered the leather get-up with the coat. When it dropped to the floor, she had only the dog collar on.

Cole thought back to their childhood. At fifteen, before Alana and Mary had been turned out, Taneesha was already turning tricks. Her White-girl looks and liking for painful sex made her a whorehouse star.

Their secret was that, while Cole and Sugar didn't fuck with their friends that way, only with the older whores, Cole and Taneesha had always snuck around and screwed. He'd been the first to fuck her in the ass. Even her asshole stepfather, who'd taught her to like the physical abuse, hadn't done that.

Cole stripped. He stood for a few seconds, his heavy dick half-hard, and looked into her eyes. She needed this. Hell, they both did. But even Cole, vicious killer that he was, hesitated to do what he knew she wanted him to. Taneesha, sensing this, reached down and squeezed his dick. Hard.

Taking a half-step back, Cole slapped her right breast. Then the other. As her skin reddened, and the nipples sharpened into hard points, he grabbed her by the throat. The studs from the collar dug into his hand as he squeezed. He ignored the pain.

As her face darkened and she started to make choking sounds, he threw her onto the grimy carpet. Ripping her legs apart, he grabbed her ass and pulled her roughly onto his stiff dick. Taneesha groaned loudly from her sore throat as his manhood filled her.

Cole pounded her into the rough carpet, pinning her arms above her head as she bucked against him. It was rough, brutal, painful sex. Her ass and back were pounded into the hard floor. His knees were scraped as he inched forward to maintain maximum contact.

Neither of them cared. Cole could only think about the hot, wet pussy surrounding his dick. Taneesha reveled in the combined pain and pleasure he was giving her. And in the fact that it was Cole doing it. He and Sugar were the only two men in the world that she gave a shit about. If only he were here with them, splitting her ass apart while Cole beat up her pussy.

That thought pushed her over. She came, twisting her ass frenetically. Cole's seed poured into her, and her orgasm intensified. Her body was a mass of sensation. Tears flowed as their bodies continued to strain against each other. Finally, they were still.

Taneesha rubbed his back, satisfied. "Hey."

"What?"

"You know I only like to hurt while we're doing it. This floor's got cum, crack, and who knows what else. Let me up."

Cole pushed himself up and helped her to her feet. He gave a low whistle. "Damn."

She looked over her shoulder into the mirror. Her back, ass, and legs looked like somebody had beat her. Hell, usually they had.

"Let's shower and clean up. Then I'll work my phone and find out what you need to know."

Over the course of the next hour, Taneesha had gotten a wealth of information about Bullet's street activities. Cole was a little surprised to find that she had a logical, precise mind, and asked all the right questions. The tricks she called, eager to curry favor with her and knowing she was street legit, didn't hold back.

Watching her, Cole had an idea. He was still a little bothered about the way she was. It was dangerous. He and Sugar, too, he knew, only went along because it was what she wanted, and she begged them to. The miracle was, she hadn't been seriously hurt or killed by some sadistic asshole.

He sat and tore up one of the bed sheets as she wrote down the names and places she was soliciting information from. When she was done, he took the pad and pen from her hand.

"Lie down. On your back."

Taneesha gave him a puzzled look, then complied. Her little self-satisfied smile gave away the fact that she thought Cole was about to reward her with some of the rough sex she liked so much.

Using the strips of linen, Cole bound her to the bed by her wrists and ankles. Last of all he used a strip to blindfold her.

"You've got to be quiet," he said. "Are you going to do this my way, or do I have to gag you too?"

Trembling with anticipation of whatever kinky idea he had, Taneesha nodded, her loins already getting hot. Cole drank in the sight of her. The darker shade of skin around her nipples, and the slight broadening of her nose and lips were the only real indications that she had Black blood.

"You know, you're a beautiful woman." He spoke softly as he knelt on the bed.

He gently kissed the corners of her mouth with soft, feather-light touch, letting their breaths mingle. Inserting his tongue between her lips, he prodded them open and kissed her deeply, while running his hands back and forth down her sides, from hips to armpits.

Taneesha was surprised. As many times as she'd had sex since her early teens, she had never been kissed like this. Cole's hands brushing the bottoms of her breasts in their roaming felt good. When he took her nipples between his fingers, she tensed, waiting for the familiar pain that never came.

When he laid his palm on her mound, his fingers curled around her pussy lips, her hips jerked. "Cole? What . . ."

"Sssh. No talking. Remember?"

When she nodded, he lowered his head, licking her nipples one at a time, occasionally pulling at them with his lips. Taneesha's thoughts whirled. What was he doing? From her first time, at thirteen, she'd been handled roughly during sex.

Armond alternated between rape, beatings, threats, and bribes until her young head was all fucked-up. She would do anything to please him. She soon equated pain with sexual pleasure, to the point she asked for it from him and all the ones after.

She pulled at her bonds, wanting to scratch and bite him so he'd hurt her, then fuck her. His forefinger gently touched her lips.

"Sssh."

Cole lifted her hips and lowered his face. Spreading her pussy lips with his tongue, he licked her salty slit. Taneesha's juices poured from her. He sucked and licked her clitoris mercilessly, until she jerked her hips, moaning softly.

Sensing her impending orgasm, he prodded her wet slit with his dick.

"Oh, Cole. Baby, please!"

He entered her with one quick thrust. Taneesha screamed as she came. Cole thrust into her over and over. When he couldn't take it anymore, he poured himself into her. Supporting his weight on his elbows, he continued to kiss her and nuzzle her throat and breasts until she lay still, her chest heaving.

"Can I talk now?"

At his nod, she continued. "Why did that never work before? It's never been that good. I had to have the pain to come. What did you do to me?"

"I didn't do nothin'. You're a beautiful, sexy woman. If you want to hustle tricks, okay. I was just a dumb, horny kid when we were young. I tried to give you what you wanted. You don't need all that bullshit to get off."

She was silent for a while. Cole realized she was crying when he noticed the wetness on her blindfold. He loosened her bonds and held her while she clung to him.

"Thank you."

"What're friends for? I got to go, baby. Gotta meet Sugar and Jess at the old place. First, I need to make a few stops."

Taneesha saw that all of a sudden the old Cole was back. The one with the empty eyes. When he came out of the bathroom and started to get dressed, she gave him the list she'd made. "I won't tell."

"What?"

"That you're an undercover lover."

He laughed at her jibe. "Ain't no secret. I taught Sugar all he knows. You just stay on The Strip till we call you. Bye, baby."

He left to do his thing.

CHAPTER THIRTY-THREE

The three main sources of legal income along the Mississippi Coast were the fishing industry, the military, and the casinos. The Back Bay of Biloxi practically overflowed with shrimp and fishing boats. It was not uncommon for a shrimper to leave the harbor well before dawn, and to have worked his boat to the Yucatan Peninsula and back before midnight.

Of course, this made shrimpers very attractive to drug smugglers. The value of the dope smuggled into the Back Bay easily exceeded the revenues of all three of the legitimate coast income sources combined. And the drug business along the coasts of Mississippi, Alabama, and Louisiana was rising steadily.

Bullet was a cruel, violent psychopath, true, but he was far from stupid. Even as a young hustler, he had an intuitive grasp of the overall picture of the drug business. This had made him determined to be more than just a Black street hustler. So far, the events of the last couple of days seemed more and more like the opportunity he needed to leap to the level of the top players.

He knew all about the war years ago between the Cali and Medellin cartels. After unifying in the eighties to import more than ninety-five percent of the cocaine arriving into America, there had been a falling out and constant warfare between Escobar, the head of the Medellin group, and the Rodriguez brothers, leaders of the Cali.

After Escobar's death in 1993, the Cali cartel's imports into America jumped from twenty-five percent to eighty percent. This alerted the narcs, and the brothers were pursued and hounded until their deportation and sentencing a couple of years ago. This left a huge vacuum in the cocaine trade. And billions upon billions of dollars up for grabs.

The Mexicans had stepped up in a big way. The Tijuana, Sinaloa, Juarez, and Gulf cartels had formed and were importing vast amounts of powder. They mostly stuck to the old tried-and-true methods and routes used by their former bosses, the Cali and Medellin cartels. The Puerto Ricans had also become players.

To avoid a war, the Ricans had concentrated on the more sparsely populated and under-enforced Mississippi coastal region. And they were coming up. Bullet was determined to come up with them. Right now, he had forty-seven million dollars in an account in Antigua, which he'd accumulated over the last ten years. If things worked out for him today, he could double it or more by this time next year.

As they cruised the waterfront in North Biloxi, he instructed Trey. "Go to the Marina over by Popp's Ferry. There's a big yacht there Cisco used to mention. I don't know the dude, but he's the one we got to see."

The Puerto Rican's boat wasn't hard to spot. Not only was it the biggest one there, but the men posted front and back looked just like what they were—guards. Bullet and

Trey parked and walked slowly down the dock, their hands empty and held well away from their bodies.

The man at the bottom of the gangplank hailed them. *"Hola,* homeboys. What you doin' here?"

"I came to see the man," said Bullet. "My name is Bullet, an' I worked for Cisco. I need instructions."

The guard looked at him a long time. "Wait right here. Don't move. I'll see if he will talk to you."

He motioned with his hand, and another man, this one holding a pistol at his side, came down the gangplank. The first man went onto the boat. Three minutes later, he was back. He waved Bullet and Trey up.

"Just you." The man pointed to Bullet. "Your friend can wait right here."

Bullet followed the man down the steps and into a plush cabin. A slim Hispanic man dressed in a bathrobe sat at a small table. A larger man holding an assault rifle stood near the bar, and the guard who'd led him here remained in the doorway.

"I am Oscar Fuentes. You wanted to see me?"

"They call me Bullet. I would not bother you, but I had no choice. Francisco is dead. So is Jesse Verdun. I have worked with them a long time, but I need to know where I stand, or if I need to find new people."

Fuentes looked into Bullet's eyes a long time. His stare was penetrating, and Bullet started to sweat. Nothing and nobody scared him, but he knew that if this man had even the slightest suspicion that he was responsible for Cisco and Jesse's deaths, he would never leave there alive.

"Have a seat, Bullet. We do have much to discuss."

Bullet sat, suppressing his relief. Damn, he missed Ace.

"Cisco has indeed spoken of you. He was about to

leave the business, and he had recommended that your role be increased. Your volume is steadily increasing, and you have the connection with the local police that can help us all. Like you, I know that the product must continue to move."

The man's eyes grew hard. "When I find out who killed Cisco, Alana, and Jesse, I will handle it. This is what you will do. I will arrange for one hundred kilos to be delivered to you. You will pay me one million dollars. By the time this product is gone, I will have solved our problem, and we will discuss further arrangements."

Fuentes motioned to the man behind him. A small device was handed to Bullet.

"This is a phone which will connect you to someone who works for me. Use it for nothing else. He will instruct you on how to receive your product and how to deliver my money. Do you understand and accept my terms?"

Bullet's heart was pounding. A hundred birds! He would easily clear a couple mil' off this one deal! Of course, he understood what had not been said. This was his chance to be accepted into the upper echelons of the Puerto Rican cartel.

"Yes, I do. Also, I will use all my connections to assist in findin' out what happened to Cisco. He was always straight with me. I appreciate what you are doing for me, and I will show you what I can do."

Fuentes nodded, but he continued to watch Bullet with that disconcerting stare.

When Bullet regained the upper deck, he breathed a sigh of relief. Trey looked at him expectantly.

"Let's go. We're gonna own this town and everybody in it."

When Bullet left, Oscar spoke again. "Enrique, set this

up. Meanwhile, continue to dig into the truth of what happened to Cisco and Jesse. It is very convenient for this Bullet that they both died so close together, no?"

"I am not sure. What I do know is that I want to find out exactly what happened. Maybe someone else is trying to move in on our operation. I have made some calls. Francisco was my blood. Someone will pay for his life."

CHAPTER THIRTY-FOUR

Cole turned left off Main Street onto Division. The drive through the old neighborhood stirred up a lot of dormant memories. His interlude with his old girlfriend had been fun and satisfying, as well as informative. Now, though, it was time to get it on. To do what he did best. He had carefully studied the sheet of information Taneesha had compiled for him.

Cole had never bothered to try and understand what it was inside him that made it so easy for him to kill. Maybe his nightmare of a childhood, with a whore for a mother, no father, and no one else but Sugar and their young girls. Maybe he was just bent.

Whatever it was, it made no difference now. Bullet had killed Alana. He was trying to kill Jessica and Sugar. He needed to know that it would cost him to fuck with Cole's people. Yeah, he was anxious to see Sugar and Jess, but first he wanted to even the odds a bit.

On the corner of Haise and Bradford streets sat a crack house run by Bullet's men. He turned onto Haise from Division and pulled over. His modified Calico machine pistol could spit fifty rounds in a few seconds. The two Glocks attached to the leather harness would add thirty-four more.

Parking on the street three houses down from his target, he watched the old wood-framed place for a while. This early in the afternoon business was slow, and in twenty minutes only two customers showed up. The first, holding his hand in his pocket and looking around nervously, knocked on the door and was admitted.

The next was a skinny girl. She was inside for less than a minute. Coming back out, she hurried away, head down and almost running. The first guy hadn't come out at all. *Smoking his rock,* Cole thought.

Sticking the hand holding the Calico inside a brown paper bag, Cole got out and casually walked up onto the porch. He knocked three times.

"Yo," was the reply.

"I need a fifty pack."

The moment the door started to open, Cole kicked it hard. The man behind it was still falling away when Cole shot him, the bullets making him jerk like a puppet. Before he hit the floor, Cole was over him and inside the room.

He shot the man against the far wall, and ignored the one still holding the pipe. His eyes were bugged, but he never stopped working the flame. The filthy kitchen was empty, so Cole retraced his steps and entered the short hallway. Two of the rooms had no doors, and there were sounds coming from the one at the end.

Cole started firing three feet from the door. Dropping the Calico, he ripped both nines from the harness. He didn't need them. The bloody guy on the bed had picked the wrong time to get a blow job.

His torso was a mess from throat to groin. The girl was somehow still between his legs in a grotesque parody of sex. The back of her head was gone. After a glance to make sure there was no one else, Cole quickly went back the way he'd come.

The crackhead in the living room looked like he was having a heart attack. The pipe lay broken on the table and his eyes were wide with fear.

"Don't shoot me, man. I just came to buy some dope."

"What's your name?"

"Pook."

"Well, Pook, you tell Bullet or somebody that works for him that Cole came by. Sugar's friend. You do that for me?"

"Yeah, bro. Anything you say."

"Pook, you deliver my message. Be sure to do that. Better grab what you can and get ghost. Cops gonna be here soon."

And he was gone.

Pook grabbed the bag of rocks and a wad of cash from the pockets of Joey, the man dead in the doorway. Then he took Cole's advice.

Chapter Thirty-Five

Jessica sat in a Starbuck's coffee house just off the 110 interchange. She was scared shitless, but this was a chance she felt she had to take. Nora had given her Sugar's foreign account number after their talk. With no working phone lines at the warehouse, and being unsure whether or not she could access the internet with her cell, she needed a computer with an internet connection.

Once she got her nerves under control, stealing Bullet's money was easy. She got his bank, gave the proper code words, and put all but one hundred thousand into Sugar's Belize account. Forty-seven million dollars! Shit. She knew he was raking it in, but forty-seven mil'? Bullet?

Another thing that amazed her was the fact that, for years, almost all of the money Sugar collected from his Game was put into the Belize account by Elnora. Hell, the girls never bothered to wonder what Sugar did with the money. Their men took care of them, and even if they hadn't, Sugar would always give them whatever they wanted.

The Game was their way of holding on to their ties together. To who they had been, and in fact, still were.
Now, it had brought them to this. And took Alana from
them. Because of Bullet.

She was tempted to call the asshole and let him know
how she had fucked him over. That would be stupid,
though. Let Sugar and Cole handle him. They would
protect her. They always had.

Sipping her latte, she thought about her talk with Nora.
She felt guilty that she had known her, been close to her so
long, but had never really seen her. Was she really that selfish and shallow? But, shit, Sugar was just as guilty as
she was, wasn't he?

One thing was sure, though. Nora loved him. Really
loved him. The question was, did Jessica herself truly
love Sugar? She had always thought she did. He made
her feel safe. He saw her and treated her as a real person.
No, a real special person. And he fucked her stupid every
time.

But was that really love she felt? To tell the truth, she
felt the same way about Cole. Except the sex, and that
was 'cause he had been gone so long. Ever since they
were kids, for her, Lana, Mary, and Taneesha, Sugar and
Cole had been their men. No matter who they were
"with" at the time.

Jessica had always been a fighter. Trouble was, right
now she wasn't sure if she really wanted to fight Nora for
Sugar. Or if she would win if she did. That little bitch was
something else when she dropped her disguise.

Well, almost time to go back.

She pulled out her phone and dialed. "Hey. It's me.
Where the hell are you? What! You been here that long
and didn't come see me. Us? And you been with Neesha?
I'm mad at you. What? At Starbucks in the old strip center. Yeah, where the Magic Johnson Theatres are. I don't

care. John Coleman, you bring that fine ass right here. Right now! Bye."

She was smiling as she disconnected. Cole never could handle her. She was always the only person, besides maybe Sugar, who could order him around. And she knew it.

Flipping open her phone again, she called Nora and told her she was waiting for Cole to pick her up. He had a lot of information for them and he wanted Sugar and Nora to sit tight until they got there, no matter how long it took.

Just talking to Cole had changed her whole attitude. Now that he was here, anyway. That nigga Bullet thought he was pissed about her and Sugar. Wait till her and Cole got through with him.

Jessica, you one treacherous bitch, she thought.

"Yeah, and I'm about to hook up with one dangerous-ass nigga," she answered herself.

She laughed out loud when she realized her loins were tingling with anticipation. Ten minutes later, Cole walked in. Since she hadn't told him she was seated at a computer carrel, it took him a while to find her. She studied him.

He looked the same, yet different, slim and brown-skinned. She knew that his clothing concealed a well-built body. Hair cut short, and dressed in black. Jessica found herself liking the way he looked. She stood up. The way his eyes lit up when they landed on her and roamed her body made her feel that tingle again.

She went to him and looked up at him.

"What's up, baby girl? I see you still the baddest bitch of them all."

"So you say, nigga. Come here, boy."

He wrapped her in his arms. Gently he kissed both cheeks and brushed her lips. "Miss me?"

"I'm still mad at you. Let me find out you been fuckin'

Taneesha. Y'all think nobody knew you two was screwin' when we was kids, huh?"

Cole recovered quickly. "Why you worried 'bout Neesha? You was always sweet on Sugar."

"That's 'cause you kept runnin' from me."

"Hold up, ma. This nigga ain't never run from nothin'."

"Bullshit. Come on."

As she led the way back to her table, Jessica could feel his eyes burning into her ass. Her and Cole had always flirted and played like this. How come she got the feeling that now neither one of them was joking? They sat down.

"Talk to me, baby girl. What's up?"

Chapter Thirty-Six

Nora hung up the phone after her conversation with Jessica. She had just come from her shower and was getting dressed in the old bedroom that had once belonged to Taneesha and Alana. Dropping her towel, she studied her naked body in the full-length mirror on the closet door.

In her senior year of high school, going steady with Abu, she had known she was beautiful. Abu told her that constantly, and she could not walk down the halls without attracting looks, leers, whistles, and propositions. She had been proud of her body and her looks. Tight jeans, short skirts, and revealing blouses had ensured that everybody noticed her.

Then came the rape and Abu's murder. Ever since, she had gone out of her way to conceal the way she looked. Her mind and her emotions had shut down. Fear ruled her life. Her world had consisted of one solid object for years. Sugar.

Maybe, she thought, if she had gone to the shrinks and

counselors Sugar suggested, they could have helped her. But she'd refused, hiding herself totally away from the world that had damaged her so. Except for him. He had saved her. He had become her life.

When had the fog cleared? When had she come awake and started to feel again? Even she didn't know. Was it when she realized that, despite the sexual games he played with the girls, Sugar truly cared for them all? And the big question: When did she realize that she truly loved him and wanted him for herself? That way?

Nora shuddered at the thought of physical intimacy. In contradiction, her nipples grew hard as she watched, and she felt a heat descend into her lower belly. There was no denying that her body was alive again. And it was still a beautiful body, she had to admit.

Her breasts were high and full, her stomach flat. The thick bush between her legs leaked moisture from its center. Her firm calves rose to perfectly proportioned thighs and a gorgeous round ass. Her body could compete with them all—except for maybe Alana's.

But could she do this? She could only hope and pray that her mind didn't rebel and retreat into hiding. That she wouldn't be frigid. It would ruin everything. And why would Sugar want her, when he had all the others? For years she had heard their joyous cries during sex.

"Stop it!" she told herself. Alana was dead. They all might be soon. In just a few hours. More than anything, she wanted Sugar to see her. To desire her. To love her. And dammit, she was going to have him. And right now!

Sugar sat straight up in bed when the door slammed open. The hand holding the pistol he'd snatched from beneath the pillow went limp as his eyes opened in shock.

Nora stood in the doorway, dressed in some kind of sheer nightgown.

Her long hair was down around her shoulders, and she stood, legs slightly apart and backlit from the light in the room behind her. The sight literally took his breath away. Most surprising, though, was the look on her face. Her jaw was set in determination, and she looked him square in the eye.

"We need to talk."

"Nora! Baby, are you all right?"

The real question was apparent in his voice and expression. He was wondering if she had completely snapped.

"Yeah. I'm okay, Sugar. Alana's dead. Somebody's trying to kill us. Jessica is meeting Cole to try and figure out how to kill them first, but yeah. I'm okay, for the first time in a lot of years. And we need to talk."

Not a whole lot in the world could shock Sugar into inaction. His survival and success proved that. But this version of Nora set him back on his heels. "Oh. Okay. Come sit down. Tell me what's on your mind."

She swayed over and sat on the edge of the bed. Up close, he could see and feel her nervousness.

"Stop staring at my titties. We can talk about those later. This is important."

He jerked his eyes up to meet hers. It was as if she'd slapped him. Nora? His Nora said that? He tried to ignore the tingle in his groin. For all these years, ever since he had found those pigs rutting and slobbering over her, Sugar had known what a fine, beautiful woman Nora was. Maybe she hid it from the rest of the world, but he'd known better.

Time and time again, at first, he had tried to help her

get over the trauma. He had failed each time. Finally he had backed off and let her find her own way to deal with it. He'd also suppressed his desire for her. For her sake. But now she was pressing. He hoped she knew what she was doing.

Chapter Thirty-Seven

"And that's it, up to now."

Jessica had told Cole a condensed version of all that had happened. Including the game they had all played with Sugar.

"You know him. He'll stand up and fight anybody, anytime. One-on-one, I'd bet on Sugar, but Bullet's got an army."

"He *had* an army. Besides, that's not what I meant.

"Oh." Her cheeks reddened. "I'll be straight-up with you. I carried a torch for you, for a long time. You left, and I focused all my affection on Sugar. But I've always known, even as sweet as he is to me, and as close as we are, that he don't love me that way. After talking to El-nora, I think she may be the reason.

"I need somebody, Cole. Somebody who really cares about me. More than just a bad bitch with some good pussy. I want a life. Children. I'm so tired of this shit."

Cole looked at her beautiful face, at the tears she barely held in check. "Look, Jess. You got to know the way I've always felt about you. It had a lot to do with me putting off coming home. For one thing, Sugar is my boy. I always assumed that you and him . . . well, you know.

"Another is what I am. You know me. I don't take no shit and I could give a damn about wasting some asshole. Most of them need it. Maybe I'm wrong, but it's who and what I am. A killer. What woman could deal with that? I've had a lot of women, but it's all temporary. They all end up scared of me. Of what I am."

"Do I look like a lot of women to you, Cole?"

"Naw, but—"

"But what? You, of all people, know me. Where I, where we all came from. And I, of all people, other than Neesha maybe, know that inside that killer is a man. A good man."

"Jess, be for real. Do you really think you can handle who I am? What I do?"

"We'll know in a little while. I'm going with you."

"Bullshit! Girl, I ain't taking no chance on you catching a bullet meant for me. This shit is for real."

"Who do you think you're telling? I can take care of myself. I can shoot. Sugar taught us all. That asshole killed my friend. Besides, you don't know what it was like, how he treated me.

"What do you think I did when Alana called me? If I could have been sure he was alone, I would have waited and killed him myself. I called you and Sugar, then I hit him where it really hurts."

"What you talking about?"

"I took his money. All of it. We're all rich. You got about ten million dollars coming. You want to take it and walk away?"

Cole was shocked. She was serious.

"You know the answer to that. Ten millon! I guess you

are tougher than you look. Jess, you sure you want to do this? You don't have to, and I'll come for you anyway when I'm done, money or not."

"Baby, I got to do it. You need to know that I can handle your world. I need to do something myself to put all this shit behind me. Besides, I lived with that nigga all those years. I know most of his people and his spots. I can help."

Cole sat back and blew a sigh. "All right. I knocked off a crack house a while ago over on Haise. I told a crack-head to tell Bullet I was coming for him. My plan is to hit as many of his workers as I can before I go get Sugar, then together we'll finish it. The odds will be a lot better then."

"Sounds good to me. I'll call Nora and tell her I'll be with you. We'll let them know we're coming when we get done. All right?"

"Let's go."

Jessica rose and followed him out to his car. She was scared as hell. She hoped she hadn't let her mouth write a check her ass couldn't cash.

It was a world of difference between letting Cole and Sugar protect her ass and being right there doing the shooting herself.

But she knew she needed to do this. For herself, yes, but definitely if she wanted a chance at a future with Cole. He needed to know she didn't fear or despise him for the violence he lived with. By the time she took a seat beside him in the car, she was ready.

For the next two hours or so they rained bullets and blood all over central Biloxi. Jessica directed Cole to a corner of Forrest Avenue. Bullet's workers sold crack along a whole block. In the early darkness, Jessica fired round after 9 mm round into the slingers as Cole sped up the block. Most scattered, but she saw four of them fall.

At the corner of La Salle, he took a right and parked. "In ten minutes, pick me up at the corner of F Street and Forrest," he said. Then he was gone.

Jessica moved over and sat anxiously the whole time, listening for police sirens and hearing faint sounds that could have been gunshots. When she reached the corner, she didn't see Cole. The passenger door opened suddenly, and he was there.

This pattern, or a variation on it, was repeated on Hoxie, Collier, Ahern, Copp, Lee, and at several crack houses. Jessica finally understood some of what Cole meant. He was a killer. A killing machine. And she did her part too. By the time they were ready to head to the warehouse and Sugar, Bullet was twenty-two men short, and they were bonded together in blood.

Chapter Thirty-Eight

"I'm scared, Sugar," Nora began. "Tonight I had a long talk with Jessica while you were sleeping."

"What did y'all talk about?"

"About what happened when, you know . . . you saved me. And about the Game." She took a deep breath and continued. "I never talked about that to anybody. Not even to you. I didn't even allow myself to think about it. Except in my dreams.

"You don't know, can't even imagine, what it's been like for me. I panic, get chills whenever you are out of my sight or hearing. Do you know I used to stand outside the door when you were with the girls? I would hear you making love to them, and even that was okay, as long as I knew you were there. How sick is that?

"But lately, over the last few months, things started to change. It began to bother me to hear you screwing them. I even began to wish it was me in there."

Nora hung her head in shame, unable to go on.

"Sometimes—most times—I wished it were you too," Sugar said softly.

Nora jerked her head up and met his eyes. "Really?"

"Nora, you just don't know how really beautiful and special you are. Not just on the outside, but inside. I'm sorry. I know that over the years I've taken you for granted. You were always there. Always willing to do any and everything for me, most times before I could even ask.

"And this mess we're in. It's all my fault. I was selfish. The truth is, I feel like I'm no better than a pimp. I let them fuck all their men and bring me the money. Yeah, it started out as a game, but I grew to like it too much. I should have stopped it long ago. And you. I made you a promise a long time ago. To protect you. To never let anybody hurt you again.

"I should have insisted that you get professional help a long time ago. You would have done it for me. Truth is, I was scared I would lose you. Sometimes it is so hard to see you and know I can never touch you. I've been selfish. You don't have to do this. You've got enough money to do anything you want to."

"Oh, Sugar. Don't think like that. It's not your fault. The girls needed the Game, and you did too. It's not your fault, or mine. Nor Jessica's, Alana's, Mary's, Neesha's, or Shay's. It's Bullet. He killed her. He's the one who wants to kill you and Jessica. I just want you to hold me, to love me."

Sugar reached out to her, and she came into his arms. As she laid her head on his chest, they both sighed in contentment. It felt so good, so right. He wondered to himself if he had known all along that she was the one. Sugar's world hadn't left much room for gentleness and compassion.

Survival on the streets demanded a toughness and often ruthlessness that precluded any show of weakness. Only with his girls, playing the Game, could he be relaxed enough to lower his guard. With Cole it was different. They were men. He knew Cole had his back—would even die for him, and vice versa. They didn't need to talk about it or show their feelings.

Sorrow and regret filled him. Here was a woman; a beautiful, fine creature with a heart of pure gold. Nora had suffered so much, yet he knew she would give up her life for his with no hesitation. She trembled with fear, and the effort it took to be intimate, even with him, was evident in every line of her body. He wondered if he even deserved it.

Sugar pulled her head closer to his chest and rocked her gently back and forth like a child. He crooned to her softly all the while, telling her how beautiful she was, how kind and selfless he found her. Over and over he apologized for waiting so long to see her as she was. He painted a picture of their future together, promising to cherish her and protect her always.

Gradually, her shaking stilled, and he could feel her breath soft and warm against his chest. Deliberately, he pushed all thoughts of their situation, of Alana, Bullet, even the girls away. Inhaling deeply, he breathed in the strawberry scent of her hair, giving in to the soft but firm feel of her flesh as his hands stroked her back and sides.

Taking her by the shoulders, he pushed her away a little, so he could look into her eyes. The fear was still there, but there was something else too. "Nora," he breathed softly.

Softly, he brushed his lips against hers, holding the touch and letting their breaths mingle. He held himself still until he felt the pressure against his lips increase as she sought to deepen the kiss. He tongued her lips apart and kissed her for real.

His hands roamed her body as their tongues dueled. Brushing the bottoms of her breasts, the top of her ass, the backs of her knees, her lower stomach, barely touching her pubic hair. As Sugar kept his hand moving, Nora began to groan low in her throat.

The sensations she felt now were alien to her. Until the brutal rape, her only sexual experience had been with her young boyfriend. And Abu had never made her body feel like it was on fire as Sugar's touch did now. Her fears were being rapidly banished by his touch and kiss.

She gasped when he broke the kiss and moaned again when his lips found the pulse at her neck, sucking gently. Her big, round nipples were so tight, they hurt. When Sugar's lips found one, her loins tightened and liquid gushed. "Aaahh . . . ."

He played her body like a violin. His hands and lips were everywhere, it seemed. She was on fire. When he cupped her ass and lifted her pussy to his tongue, the first orgasm ripped through her. She twisted and turned, her thighs locked against his face.

"Sugar. Sugar. Oh, baby!"

He listened to her repeat his name in passion, barely able to hold his mouth to her shuddering body. He'd done it! Now she was ready for him.

His dick hurt. Holding his desire in check had been hell. He smiled as he rose to his knees between her legs.

"Are you ready?"

When she looked at the size of his dick waving back and forth, the fear almost resurfaced. But her pussy was on fire and she had to have more. She nodded her head.

Sugar bent her knees back almost to her shoulders, opening her groin to him. The big head of his dick touched her hot, pink opening, and he pushed. There was some pain; he could see her grimace slightly. Moving slowly, a fraction of an inch at a time, he filled her. When most of him was inside her, he stopped.

In seconds her body adjusted to his invasion. Her

juices coated him, and she waited for him to move. He didn't. When he bent to take her nipple into his mouth again, she couldn't take it anymore. She raised her hips. At her signal, Sugar started to move.

He fucked her slowly, amazed at how tight and hot she was. They moved in perfect synchronization for what seemed like forever. He drove into her again and again. They both felt the fluttering in her lower belly at the same time.

Sugar fucked faster, pumping into her with abandon. Nora's body went rigid as she came again. When her hot vagina started to convulse around him, he let out a loud moan and emptied himself into her. They thrashed, pushing and clutching at each other with unbridled passion.

Spent, they lay tightly wrapped in each other's arms. In slightly different words, they were both thinking the same thing. Their lives, their whole world had changed. Sex was a joining of the bodies involved. This was much more. This had joined them spiritually. Forever.

CHAPTER THIRTY-NINE

Bullet was beside himself with rage. He killed the cell phone transmission and threw the phone on the table. He paced the long width of the upstairs room in the crack house. Suddenly he stopped, picked up one of the big Pyrex dishes used to cut up dope, and hurled it against the barred window. It shattered into a million pieces, startling Trey, who leaned against the far wall.

"Fuck! Those motherfuckin' pussy-ass niggas are pissin' me off!"

"What happened?"

"That damn Cole and some bitch been knockin' off our people. Both in the houses and on the corners."

After leaving the docks and Oscar Fuentes, the two men had returned to the house on Nixon Street. Bullet was ecstatic that he had cut a deal with the Puerto Ricans that would put him on top. All he had to do was wait on the call and take delivery of the hundred kilos.

The dope house was a fortress. Even the cops would have a hard time taking it out if he had enough men to defend it. So he'd made a plan. It was simple. Get Farelli, and the cops to take Coleman, and he and his boys could handle Sugar and Jessica. Hire more men and blanket both Biloxi and Gulfport with the kilos.

While the people who worked for Jesse in Gulfport were disorganized, it would be easy. He'd run it all in no time. It had been less than twenty-four hours since he'd killed Cisco and Alana to start all this. He'd recovered well and turned it all to his advantage, except for Ace. Man, did he need him now.

"That was Farelli. I paid him a mil' to give us one day to make our move. We still got six or seven hours left. But that nigga Cole, Sugar's boy, rolled in from H-town with some ho an' they been knocking off our people.

"If they keep this up, we won't be able to move the shit fast enough here, let alone Gulfport. That nigga's a real bad-ass, psycho motherfucker. I think they still want him for an old killin' here, so I wanted Farelli to take him out. That cracker's tellin' me that the bodies are attracting too much attention.

"A full-scale drug war's gonna bring in the Feds for sure an' the National Guard maybe. We got to end this shit quick and fade till Farelli can put it all on the Ricans and make it old news. Trouble is, I don't know where Sugar, Cole, an' that bitch are, so I can't do nothin'!"

"What's Fuentes gonna think when the laws put on the heat?"

"I don't give a shit. The dope is gonna keep coming. Our problem is them niggas."

Trey held his tongue. The way he saw it, the problem was Bullet's temper. His killing Cisco and Alana started all this shit. Hell, Sugar wasn't even in the dope game. And everybody knew Cole was bad news. Pussy was pussy. You didn't fuck up your cash flow behind a piece. You just got a new piece.

Wisely though, he didn't say any of this. Not only was he a soldier, he was a soldier about to get a real big promotion.

"I talked to Brew. They went by Sugar's restaurant and by that broad Mary's place. The rib joint is closed, and nobody was home at Mary's. Hold on. I got an idea."

Trey whipped out his own phone and dialed. He had figured out how to find Sugar a while ago. First, though, he let Bullet do it his way. Now he would show his worth as Ace's replacement.

"Brew. Trey. Listen. Y'all go to The Strip and find a broad named Taneesha. Yeah. That one. Looks like a White girl. Be careful, but whatever it takes, grab her and bring her to Nixon. Don't fuck her up. Later."

He looked up into Bullet's puzzled eyes. "Sugar and Cole hung around with a bunch of hoes from The Strip. They all was raised over there. That's why they all so tight. This bitch Taneesha is Sugar and Jessica's friend, Cole too. If we have her, they'll come to us and deal. You okay with that? "

Bullet broke into a huge smile. "Boy, you a genius! We can settle this shit with them niggas, I can get the bitch and my money back, and we start to roll. Good lookin'."

Chapter Forty

When Cole and Jessica entered the warehouse loft, Cole reached out and grabbed her arm. "Sssh," he said, putting a finger to his lips.

Jessica had been about to call for Sugar and Nora, but she obeyed Cole and froze, listening for trouble. She could barely hear a faint, rhythmic sound, but couldn't identify it. Not at first. As she followed Cole's silent steps across the living area, the sounds became clearer. She smiled.

The door to Sugar's room stood open, and the sight that greeted them when they stepped around the corner held them mesmerized. Nora was on her knees, her ass tilted in the air. Sugar was behind her, fucking her like a pile driver.

Jessica could see his thick dick, slimy with their juices, as it slid in and out of Nora. Each time his groin met her ass, she grunted. Her face was a picture of carnal ecstasy. Jessica's panties grew wet instantly.

Cole couldn't help but admire Nora's body. She was a

golden angel with perfect proportions. Her breasts jiggled with each stroke and she and Sugar were totally lost in their own world. He stood entranced until Jessica's fingertips brushed his hard cock.

When he glanced over at her, she turned and walked away. He followed, his dick rock-hard now, made more so by the way she exaggerated the sway of her hips. She stopped near the sofa and started to remove her clothes. Cole was no fool, and by the time she kicked her panties away, he stood naked, his desire evident.

Jessica gave him a sexy smile, and then turned her back to him. Kneeling on a futon in front of the TV, she looked over her shoulder at him, then lowered her forehead to her crossed arms. Her ass twitched.

Cole had been caught up in the beauty of her body, so much like he'd imagined over the years. The pink cleft of her sex drew him like a magnet. He quickly knelt behind her, rubbing his dick up and down her slit until he was coated with her juices.

Jessica rocked back and forth, pushing her ass at him, begging for penetration. He obliged. He slid his full length into her in one long stroke.

"Mmph."

That was the only sound she made. Cole began to stroke her. Her ass felt so good in his hands. He watched her butt flatten slightly each time he went in. Reaching around, he pinched her hard nipples.

Jessica rolled her ass in circles, occasionally stopping to clench her cheeks, tightening herself around him. Except for sometimes with Sugar, it had never been like this for her. She was on fire. She increased her backward pushes, and Cole instantly understood what she wanted.

Placing both hands around her waist, he began to fuck her hard, slamming his dick through the slight resistance of her tight pussy. Their flesh slapped together over and over. Neither realized how loud it sounded, or how long they had been at it.

Jessica froze and moaned, "Now, baby. I'm ready."

Cole could feel her pussy start to flutter around him. He increased the pace, straining toward his own release. They exploded into orgasm, him right behind her. Their groins ground and twisted together as he poured himself into her. The applause startled them.

When they whirled around, Jessica saw Sugar and Nora, her wrapped in a sheet and him with boxers on, grinning and clapping. At least, she was pretty sure it was Nora. No glasses, hair cascading over her shoulders, smiling mischievously, a voluptuous body not quite hidden by the sheet.

"Well, son, it looks like old Sugar taught you how to do one thing right." Sugar's mirth was barely contained.

Before Cole could respond, Jessica piped up. "As an expert and impartial witness, I can honestly say that maybe he taught you!"

"I'm no expert, but I am honest, and I say that my man could teach anybody how to do that." Nora hugged Sugar possessively.

They all looked at each other and burst out laughing.

"What's up, boy? I come all the way from Texas to save yo' ass and what do I find? You done snatched up an angel and corrupted the poor thing."

"Nora, this is Cole. Don't mind anything he says and take your eyes off his dick!"

"I wasn't . . ."

She noticed the other three laughing at her. She also noticed with relief the slight nod and smile that Sugar and Jessica gave each other.

"We'll be right back." Nora pulled Sugar toward the bathroom thinking, *Yes, he really is my man now.*

When they had all showered and dressed, Cole and Sugar sat talking in the living room while Nora and Jessica made snacks.

"You mean to tell me that Jessica helped you waste those dudes? What the fuck—"

"Hey, you the one taught them to shoot. I didn't make her into Calamity Jane."

"If she's Calamity, then I must be Annie Oakley. I can outshoot them all. Even Sugar, when we shoot at targets."

Sugar looked up and smiled as Nora and Jess walked in carrying the food. It still surprised him to hear her speak up. Her looks didn't give him pause, because he'd already known she was a knockout. But the personality change was still hard to take. Seeing the way Jessica looked at her, Sugar knew she felt it too.

"We heard you two making plans. Let's get this out of the way right now. Cole, Jessica already told you and showed you that she's down with whatever you do. Sugar, you need to know that I'm not going to let you go nowhere and do nothing if I'm not with you. I mean that. We stay together no matter what. I'll do my part."

Sugar was torn. The slight tremor in her voice toward the end of her little speech told him that she still held some of her fears and dependence on him. He was okay with that, but he didn't want her in danger. He looked over at Cole.

"This may sound funny coming from me, Shug, but you should only fight the battles you can win. You ain't gonna win this one, and I just met the lady."

Nora threw a grateful smile, which blossomed into a sunburst at Sugar's slight nod. Meanwhile, Jessica had sat in Cole's lap and was feeding him between kisses. Nora plopped herself down on Sugar's knee.

Cole pushed Jessica into the sofa beside him. "As

much as I'd like for us to kick back for a while, we got work to do. We need to finish this. Tonight."

Almost immediately a sober mood came over the whole group. They all knew that none of their newfound joy in each other would be worth a damn until Bullet was dealt with.

"We hurt his operation," Cole continued, "but now we've got to take out the head. Any ideas where he might be?"

Jessica answered. "Where else but Nixon? And it's gonna be a bitch getting to him."

Chapter Forty-One

Brew and Conch sat in the dim light of the strip joint and watched Taneesha dance. Clad only in chains and a few scraps of leather, she commanded a great deal of attention.

"Man, that bitch is fine! You sure she ain't White?"

"Naw, she Black, but she's fucked-up in the head. A real freak for pain and bondage an' shit. How much cash you got on you?"

"'Bout eight hundred. Why?"

"Give it here. I'm gonna try an' do this the easy way."

Brew got up and walked over to the door leading to the rear offices and dressing rooms. He was a pretty big dude himself, but the bouncer was huge.

"'Yo. What's up? Hey, I want to hire one of your dancers as an escort for a date."

"Yeah? Which one?"

"Taneesha."

"She already booked up. Try another."

"I want her, man. Look, I'll pay fifteen hundred right

now. Cash. Plus I'll take care of her cut. A friend told me to see her and nobody else."

"What friend?" the man asked, suspicion plain in his voice.

"John Coleman."

The bouncer stiffened. "Wait right here. Don't move." He turned and went through the door.

Five minutes later he was back. "The boss says any friend of Cole's gets preference. Why don't you go back to your table and wait? When the set is over, she'll come to you. Pay the dude behind the bar before you leave."

When her number ended, Taneesha went backstage for a few minutes, then came around the curtains.

"Go get the car. Pull up by the front door."

Conch left. Taneesha came up to Brew. "So you say you know Cole. Where you meet him?"

"In Houston. We did some work together. A couple of days ago, he found out I was coming down here. He told me to look you up. And a dude at a barbecue place called *Sugar's*?"

"Yeah. Did you know he's here now? I saw him this afternoon. I just tried to call him, but his phone is off. What's your name?"

"Jason. I wish I could talk to him. Say, I'm supposed to pay the man before we leave. I got a *G* for you for the date. You okay with that? Do I pay you now, or later? I got a room at the Big Casino on the beach. You ready to roll?"

Taneesha hesitated. This all sounded good, but a lot of shit had been playing across her mind since this afternoon. Cole had put some new shit in her life. But, fuck, a whole grand, just for herself? "Just you, right? No strange shit?"

"Baby, you ever look in that mirror behind the stage?

You banging. Nothin' but a fool mistreats a thorough-bred."

"Okay. Give me five minutes to change."

"All right. I'm going to use the men's room and pay the man."

In the restroom, Brew placed two quick calls. One to Pee-Wee and Conch out front in the Suburban, and one to Bullet at the house. When Taneesha walked backed out, dressed in a short mini-skirt, he was back at the table. Damn, she was a fine-looking woman!

Everything went smoothly until they were driving off. Pee-Wee had stopped to exit the parking lot when Conch couldn't resist anymore. He turned in his seat and ogled Taneesha in the back seat. His eyes were glued to the expanse of thigh showing beneath her skirt.

"Hey. I know you! You was with Bullet. Stop. I changed my mind. I'll get your money ba—"

Her head bounced off the window as Brew's big fist exploded against her temple. Before she could recover, he had reached onto the floor boards and retrieved duct tape and plastic ties, which he used to gag and bind her. This done, he turned on Conch.

"You fuckin' up, nigga. If I hadn't been ready, she could have bailed. She work for these rednecks down here. We got enough trouble without the Dixie Mafia on our ass. Yo' dick gonna get you killed, young nigga. Read my lips—don't fuck with her. Got it?"

Conch didn't like the way Brew was spittin' at him, but he was no fool. The big nigga could break him like a toothpick. And if Bullet found out . . .

"Got it, man. The bitch is just bad, though."

"We take care of our business with her friends, you can have a hundred hoes just as bad. Stay focused, nigga."

"I said I got it, man. Chill."

At the dope house, Brew pulled the wiggling woman from the vehicle and threw her over his shoulder like a sack of potatoes. The door opened before he reached it.

"Good job! Take her upstairs and put her in one of the bedrooms. Tie her down. Nobody fuck with her. We need her."

At Bullet's words, Brew looked over at Conch. Then he trudged up the stairs with his burden. Bullet sent Pee-Wee back out for her small purse. Dumping it on a coffee table, he pawed through the contents until he found the two items he wanted. Her cell phone and her address book. Now he was ready to end this bullshit with Sugar.

CHAPTER FORTY-TWO

Nora, Jessica, Sugar, and Cole sat around the table. Piled up in its center was enough weaponry to start a small war.

"The women can use the new Uzis. They're small, and on semi-automatic they don't move around much. Sugar, you like your pump and .45. I'll take two nines and the AR. We still got to figure the best way in."

"If me and Nora were men, baby, and were used to this kind of shit, would it make it easier to find a way in?"

"Naw, Jess. That ain't it. The place got thick steel doors, double bars on all the lower windows, and he's gonna have people upstairs with rifles waiting for us. I don't have a rocket launcher, no C-4, or grenades . . ." His voice trailed off.

Sugar knew that look. "What, man?"

"I know a dude in the Navy Construction Battalion in Gulfport. They got all kind of demolition shit down there. Trouble is, I don't know if he's still there, or if he can get it if he is. I got to try and call him."

Just as Cole reached for his phone, Sugar's rang. He picked up and answered. "Yo."

"Well, if it ain't the Sugar Daddy himself. This is Bullet. We need to talk."

"Naw. We need to meet. You killed my friend. You tried to kill me. Jessica's my friend too. You'll have to go through me to get to her."

Everybody at the table froze and stared at Sugar. He held up his hand for silence. He pushed a button and the phone switched to speaker.

"Look, I'll be straight-up. I fucked up. I felt disrespected and overreacted. Cisco pulled a gun on me. Alana was an accident. Jessica took something of mine, a black bag. You killed two of my men. Cole and that broad from Houston killed over twenty. I say, let's call it quits. Bring me Jessica and my money, and we're all even."

"What makes you think I'd hand her over to you?"

"I don't want you to just give her to me. I'll make you a trade. Listen."

"Sugar. I'm sorry. He said he was Cole's friend. Don't listen to him. Don't trust . . ."

"Do all your girlfriends talk too much? Like I said, we can make a trade. And if it helps you make up your mind, I won't hurt Jessica. She got to pay for the disrespect, but she's still my woman."

Cole's voice was like steel. "This is Cole. We'll get back to you on your deal, but hear this. If one, I do mean one, hair on Neesha's head is harmed, nothing and nobody is gonna keep me from doing you. You got my word on it."

"Oh, and Sugar? Part of the deal is that you send your pit bull back where he came from. I want this war over with. Call me." The line went dead.

"The motherfucker took Taneesha. What the fuck do I do now? If we attack the house, she'll die. Think he'll trade her for the money? No way he gets Jess."

"Sugar, didn't you listen? The asshole's lying through his teeth. Give him Jess and the money, he might let Taneesha go. Then he's going to kill you anyway, and Neesha too. And you know he'll only get his hands on Jessica over my dead body," Cole said.

"I say we give him what he wants." Everybody looked at Nora.

"Or at least make him think we are. Look, we can't get into that house. For sure not with Neesha there. So we make him come out. I don't know if he will just for Jessica and three hundred grand. We got something, though, that will bring him running, and with Taneesha. When he comes out, we kill him and everybody with him."

When everyone continued to stare at her, she blushed. "What? It'll work. It's our best chance."

Sugar said, "It's a hell of an idea, baby. But what could we possibly offer that would make him come to us?"

Jessica was smiling at Nora. She'd figured it out.

"We been so caught up in the shit going down today, I forgot that Nora is the only one who really knows, other than Cole." She looked at Sugar. "When I left, I took more than just Bullet's bag of money. I took the passcodes to his overseas bank account. That's why I was in Starbucks. I put all his money into your account in Belize. He doesn't even know it yet."

"How much?"

"Forty-seven million dollars."

"Shit. Damn straight he'll come out for that."

"Yeah, but only if we make it look like he'll get his money without us killing him. For that, I'm sure he'll let Jess and Taneesha go. That's what I meant by giving him what he wants."

"Sugar, how come you didn't tell me you hooked up with Bonnie Parker? That shit is wicked. I like it."

Nora lowered her head. "I read a lot, and it's just common sense. If we can't go get him, make him come to us. And we've got the perfect bait."

While Nora was talking, Jessica was dialing her phone.

"Bullet? It's me. Shut up and listen, motherfucker. While these dudes are arguing about how to make the trade, you do this. Call your bank in Antigua and check your balance."

She hung up and smiled. "You guys still think we're dead weight?"

Both Sugar and Cole threw up their hands in surrender.

"I stand corrected," Cole said. "You ladies are gangsta."

"Wait till you see how we're gonna do it," Nora said, her eyes twinkling.

Chapter Forty-Three

Bullet sagged back into his seat. The phone call had proven the bitch right. His account was empty! Forty-seven million dollars. Ten years. That's how long it had taken him to accumulate that much money. Ten hard years.

After Pete got busted he'd started out jacking dope houses and dealers in Mobile and Pensacola. Between those jobs and a couple of robberies, he had amassed almost sixteen million dollars. Pete showed him how to get his money to the Caribbean, and turned him on to the Puerto Ricans.

He had died eight years ago, and Bullet had been on his own, him and Ace. Bullet had been religious about putting money in the account. Not counting the cash Jessica took, he could lay his hands on maybe a mil' right now. Without that account, it was all he had. Fuck the bullshit, he had to get his money back!

Conch came out of the upstairs bathroom and heard Bullet raising hell on the phone. Trey, Brew, and Pee-

Wee were downstairs too. He couldn't help being drawn to the bedroom where Taneesha was. Bullet and Brew didn't understand. This ho was hot! His dick had been hard for the last hour.

It had taken Taneesha a few minutes to work the tape over her lips loose. When Trey had re-applied it after her conversation with Sugar, he'd been careless. She had worked it loose with her tongue and teeth. She had only drawn in a couple of deep, unobstructed breaths through her mouth when Conch stuck his head in the door.

Perfect! thought Taneesha. She had seen the hungry looks the dude had been throwing at her, and constant bulge in his pants. If she played this right, he might just be her ticket out of there. She knew they were all fucked, no matter what Sugar did.

"Hey. Can you please untie my hands? They hurt. And I got to pee. Bad. Please?"

"I'm not supposed to. What you gonna do for me if I do?"

"Baby, I promise to make you feel real good. Nobody has to know. I won't tell."

Conch was hooked. His dick throbbed like hell, but he wasn't stupid. He took his pocketknife and cut the tape binding her hands to the headboard. Keeping his gun on her, he waited until she freed herself. Then he marched her next door to the bathroom.

Dropping her panties, Taneesha threw them out to Conch. "I guess I won't be needing these for a while."

His mouth dropped open when she ran her hand lightly through her bush and squatted. When she was done, she cleaned herself and stood. "No sense in keeping these on either."

She undid her short skirt and stepped out of it. Next came the blouse. Naked, she posed with her legs slightly spread and let him take it all in. Then she walked past him, brushing his chest with her tits as she squeezed by. "Come on. I keep my promises."

Taneesha switched her ass provocatively as she walked ahead of him back to the bedroom. He was hot for her, but she wanted him on fire. She needed him to put the gun down.

When she reached the foot of the bed, she turned and knelt before him. "Let's see what you got. Damn. It's like a rock. I wonder how it tastes."

She bent and took him in her mouth. He moaned. She fondled his balls as she sucked him. Now was the time to make her move.

"I want you to do something for me. I want your dick way up inside me, but first, slap my ass. Hard. It makes me so wet. Do that for me, please."

Taneesha rose and knelt on the bed. She looked over her shoulder at him and flexed the muscles in her ass. That always knocked them dead when she was dancing, and it drove young Conch crazy. Dropping the gun beside his feet, he slapped her ass cheeks.

"Ooooh, baby. That's it. Again!"

SLAP! SLAP!

"Now. Put it in. I'm so ready, baby."

The boy was lost. He stepped forward and rammed his dick into her hot box. Two strokes and he was grabbing her hips, jerking as the cum exploded from him. Taneesha figured now was the time.

She twisted and fell off the bed. Grabbing for the gun, she thumbed the safety and tried to bring it up. The barrel caught in his pants, which were pooled around his ankles. As he fell backward, dick still spurting, Conch flailed wildly, trying to reach the pistol.

He got his hands on the barrel and twisted.

BAM!

Taneesha screamed in pain as she was thrown backward, the gun torn from her hand. When Bullet and Trey rushed through the door, the pistol was on the floor, and Conch was pulling up his pants, staring at Taneesha's still form on the bed.

Bullet took it all in with one look. The girl's naked form, bloody and gap-legged, cum still dripping from her bush, and Conch wide-eyed with shock. Picking up the gun from the floor, Bullet shot him three times. When his body collapsed, blood pooling, Trey spoke up.

"Kept telling that boy pussy was gonna be his death."

"Shit!" Bullet screamed.

Trey didn't know why the last phone call Bullet received upset him so, but he knew the girl had to die sooner or later anyway. He walked over to the bed and looked down. The slug had entered her upper left breast, and from the amount of blood seeping into the sheet, Trey figured it had passed all the way through.

He was no doctor, but he knew he had to clean the wound and stop the bleeding. "She ain't dead."

Bullet looked up eagerly. "What?"

"She's alive. Losing blood, though. I'll try and clean it and stop the bleeding. She may live long enough for you to swap her out."

"Do it."

Chapter Forty-Four

When Jessica came out of the loft looking for Cole, she found him sitting alone near the bottom of the stairs leading down to the garage floor. Sensing his mood, she almost turned and went back in. She'd made her choice back in Starbucks, though, and this came with it.

Walking down past him, she sat one riser below him and leaned back into him. "It's not your fault, you know. I know she's special to you, but don't you think she's special to me too? We've hustled together, fought together, fucked the same men for most of our lives. I'd give her my last; she can have anything I got. Except you. She's my friend."

"I know all that, ma. Neesha's only a small part of what's bothering me. I know we're going to get her back. You girls came up with a heck of a plan. And I don't have to kill half of Biloxi. "That's it, though, Jess. I'm wondering, can I even do anything else? Can I stop killing? Do I even want to?"

"Cole, all that shit is 'cause of me. Didn't you hear me

in the coffee shop? I don't want you to stop being you. Not for me or for anybody else. I chose you, remember? Who and what you are goes with that. I just want us to be together. If we have to go to work every now and then, so what? We can hire a nanny."

He burst out laughing and pulled her to him. "If Nora's Bonnie, you must be Ma Barker. All right, baby, let's take care of your piece-of-shit ex and we'll play it by ear from there." He pulled her to her feet, and they went back inside.

Sugar and Nora sat on the sofa. Both knew it was almost time to start moving. He wished this moment in time would never end.

"You sure you want to do it this way? It's a good plan, but a slight variation wouldn't make a difference."

"Baby, I appreciate the thought. Try to understand, Sugar, for eight years I was lost. I didn't want anything, I didn't care about anything, I didn't do anything. Now, for the first time in all those years, I want, I care. And I'll fight for what I want and care about. Those girls are all tough, all fighters. You and Cole made them that way. What am I, chopped liver?"

"Chill, baby. I said I wouldn't stop you if you were sure. Check this out, though. I love you, Nora. I want you to be with me for the rest of my life. Anything happens to you, I'm gonna lose it. Keep that in mind."

"All those years, watching what was going on around me, helping you whichever way I could, even to play The Game, I understood that we were all fucked-up one way or the other. It didn't seem right or wrong, it just *was*. As long as I was around you, I felt safe. I could function. Nothing else mattered.

"But I wasn't crazy or retarded. My mind worked. I saw how miserable and unhappy we all were inside. Me, you, all the girls. What I didn't see was that we all needed and depended on each other. The money, the things we had, they didn't really matter. The past still had us warped and twisted.

"Alana, Mary, Jessica, you, Me, even Neesha and Shay, we were all starting to see that there was something wrong, something missing in our lives. Now that I've met Cole, the same thing applies to him too. Sooner or later, something had to give.

"What's happened these last couple of days had kind of forced our hand. Nothing is ever going to be the same. The way I see it, we're fighting for our future. For me and you. For Jessica and Cole, for Mary and her family, for Neesha and Shay. For Alana. Tonight is a beginning as well as an end. We're gonna do what we have to do to protect our friends and our future."

Sugar was only a little surprised at her speech. He was beginning to see that Nora was a deep well. Under all that seeming passivity, she was as tough as any of them. And Jess, shit, she was damn near as psycho as Cole. He leaned forward and kissed her.

"Okay, li'l gangsta. Let's get the others together and do it."

When they were all gathered in the kitchen, Sugar called Bullet.

"Okay, here's the deal. In one hour, at nine o'clock, you bring Taneesha to my restaurant. I'll be waiting outside the back door, by the pits. Leave your boys at the car with Neesha and you go in. Nora will take you to Jessica.

"Right there, she'll let you see her put the money back into your account. When it's done, she'll call me. You call your boys and they give me Taneesha. You leave. Alone. Then we're done. No more beef."

He listened for a minute.

"He won't be there. He wants me to give you a message, though. He says if you do this our way and don't try to fuck us, you'll never hear from him again. If you don't, you're dead. If I were you, I'd listen. You know him."

Another pause.

"No deal. You get the forty-seven mil' and we're done. Even look cross-eyed at Jessica or Nora and the money's gone. Forever. Everybody lives or everybody dies. Your choice. What? Yeah. One hour."

Sugar hung up the phone and looked at the others.

"That motherfucker is definitely gonna try and fuck us. Let's get over there and set up. Go on down to the truck. I'm on my way."

CHAPTER FORTY-FIVE

Bullet slapped the phone down on the table. He looked up at Trey, Brew, and Pee-Wee.

"Look, there ain't but three of you left that matters. It don't mean we can't still make it work. I got to do this part first. The deal is this: Jessica took all the money out of my overseas bank account. A lot. I got to get it back."

"How come we don't do it like we said? Get them over here after that broad upstairs, kill them, and let Farelli handle Cole if we don't get him. They can't take this place. Not the two of 'em."

"I feel ya, Trey. But they ain't dumb. No way are they gonna come here. Because they got my money, they figure I'll do anything to get it back. That's how we're gonna get them."

"What about Taneesha?"

"We'll prop her up in the car. After it all goes down, she's dead anyway. Here's the deal."

Bullet recounted his conversation with Sugar. All of them knew where the barbecue place was, so he cut right to the chase.

"Pee-Wee, you take the Suburban. Back it up right to the front door, so it can't be used. Get out and post up so you can see inside. Got it?"

Pee-Wee nodded.

"Trey, you drive. Brew and the bitch will be in the back seat of the Lexus. I'll ride shotgun. When we pull around back, Sugar will be waiting for us. I'm gonna get out and talk to him. I'll tell him you two are staying with the car to make sure he don't get the girl until I get my money. Then I'm gonna go in."

Brew said, "I don't like not knowing where that nigga Cole is."

"Me neither. Thing is, though, ain't nowhere for him to hide 'cept inside. I'll make sure Sugar knows if we so much as smell him, the girl dies and the other two bitches also. He's a pussy for them hoes, so he won't take the chance.

"Once I'm sure my money is back in my account, I'm gonna cap that treacherous ho Jessica. When you hear me shoot, kill Sugar, then Taneesha. Farelli's gonna be there in two minutes. We'll have the cops watching over us until Cole is caught or run out of town.

"Then we rebuild, get the load from Fuentes, and take over. There's enough hungry youngsters out there that it won't take a week to be back up and runnin'. No competition and no loose ends."

"Seems like you got it all worked out, Bullet. Just how we gonna be set up now?"

Bullet had been expecting Trey's question. His whole power structure had collapsed. It was time to build a new one. The murders they were about to commit would tie them together forever, which wasn't necessarily a bad thing. He needed them. It was only natural that they wanted to know where they stood. He made a decision.

"When we get back tonight, this is how it's gonna be.

Each of you gets three million dollars. Cash money from my account. Trey, you'll run this house and crew like Ace did. Twenty percent of what the house takes in. Brew, you run the other house, same cut. Pee-Wee, the street crew. Twenty for you too."

The three men looked at each other and nodded. It was a new way of doing business for Bullet. But it was fair. How much they made depended on how hard and how efficiently they ran their own operations. There would be crossover business too. Together they could build an empire. And not worry about going to jail.

"Get your guns and shit together. We'll be leaving in about twenty minutes. Everybody straight on the play?"

The nods and agreements were sincere. Bullet had them fully on board. He turned and headed up the stairs.

Trey had done as much as he could with Taneesha's wound. The peroxide and bandages Pee-Wee had brought back from the drugstore had been put to good use. The dressing wasn't professionally pretty, but it was functional. The bleeding seemed to have stopped.

Taneesha was pale and semiconscious. Trey had used a liberal dusting of powder cocaine to anesthetize the wound. She had lost a lot of blood and was definitely in need of medical attention. But she was alive. That's all Bullet cared about. That she live until he was done with her.

When Trey came up, they dressed her in one of Brew's huge shirts. Gently as they could, they carried her downstairs and loaded her into the rear of the Lexus. The others piled in and they left for Sugar's.

CHAPTER FORTY-SIX

Pee-Wee pulled into the deserted parking lot of Sugar's Bar-B-Q. As he hooked the *J* turn in front of the restaurant's entrance, he saw Bullet's Lexus enter the lot and go around the building. He backed up until his rear bumper was square across the doors.

When he got out and looked at the building, he noticed something he'd never seen in all the times he had eaten here. The blinds had been lowered across all the big windows that faced the front, as well as covering the double doors. He couldn't see inside the place.

"Shit," he mumbled. Leaving the driver's door open, he leaned in and retrieved his assault rifle from the passenger footwell. Traffic was light on the street across the lot, and he had a good field of vision. Bullet's instructions were for him to watch for Cole or anyone else approaching the place. He was also to scan the interior from the front, but the blinds took care of that.

Noticing a small crack in the ones covering the left-side door, Pee-Wee stepped over and put his eye to it. Straightening, he called Bullet's cell.

"It's me. The blinds are down, but I could see inside a little. All I saw was that funny-looking girl that's always with Sugar. She's just sitting there behind the counter. Place looks empty except for her. Okay. I got the front."

He disconnected and put the phone on the driver's seat. Taking up his post, he continued to scan the area. If everything went right, this should be over soon. He fantasized about the money and women his new position would bring.

Bullet flipped his phone closed and turned slightly in the car seat. Trey was behind the wheel. Brew sat in the rear next to Taneesha, who was propped up in the corner of the seat behind Trey. She was breathing shallowly, and spots of blood dotted the bandage around her left shoulder and chest.

"Wait until I go inside the building. Then you two get out. Brew, post up on this side by the trunk. Watch the area by those pits. Trey, take your side by the front fender. When you hear me shoot, waste Sugar. When the cops pull in, drop the guns and show your hands. Don't shoot until I do. Let's do it."

Bullet got out of the car, closed the door, and walked to where Sugar stood just in front of the big meat pits, Sugar was dressed in jeans and a sweater, and didn't appear to be armed. Bullet thought, *Could this nigger be this lame?* He stopped a couple of feet away.

"Okay. I'm here. Taneesha is in the car. I'm sure you saw her when I got out. When I know my money is back in my account, I'll call out here and my boys will let her come over to you. No tricks. I got to tell you, though, she's hurt. She got shot."

Sugar tensed and his face filled with rage. Bullet put his hand up in a conciliatory gesture.

"Wait. I didn't do it. It was an accident! She'll be okay,

but she needs a doctor. It's her shoulder. Be sure you let Cole know the deal. Where is he, anyway?"

Bullet had decided to lull Sugar's suspicions by being up front about Taneesha. Hell, in a few minutes it wouldn't matter anyway. The only thing he was unsure of was if Coleman would try and interfere.

Sugar's voice was tight with anger as he spoke. "If my girl don't make it, all bets are off. I don't give a fuck how she got hurt. She had better be okay. As you can see, I kept my side of it. Cole ain't here. Nobody's inside but Nora and Jessica. She's ready to put your money back.

"About Jessica. She's like a sister to me. I really don't give a damn what went down between you two. A lot of people got fucked off behind this shit. You don't know me, and you don't know Cole. We really ought to leave it that way. Do this and back off. Your call."

"Cool by me. I got a business to run. I already made arrangements with my bank to switch accounts. I get my money, you get Taneesha, and I leave Jessica alone. That's the deal, right?"

Sugar nodded.

"Okay, where is she?"

"Just go in the back door. Elnora will show you the way to the office. Ain't nobody in the place but them two. Word. But believe me when I tell you that they both better be okay when you come out."

Bullet was from the streets and had a fine-tuned sense of danger. He looked into Sugar's eyes and felt the first tingle of doubt. Like most of the men who'd only casually seen Sugar around, Bullet had, until now, considered him a square. A Sugar Daddy, Captain Save-A-Ho kind of nigga. Cole had a rep, and it was for real. This dude had been almost invisible.

And this nigga set it off. Also there was the fact that Cole cut for him. Hard. Bullet was no coward, but as he turned away from Sugar, he began to have second thoughts about his plan. This didn't seem like the easy mark he'd prepared for.

CHAPTER FORTY-SEVEN

The big kitchen of Sugar's was dimly lit when Bullet walked in. The short woman who was Sugar's—employee? Girl? Sister?—stood near the big butcher block. He didn't know what her function was, but he did know she dressed like a Quaker. Long, shapeless dress, hair in a severe bun, and she was a scared as a church mouse.

"Where is Jessica?"

"In the office. Sugar said to show you. Come with me."

Her voice was low, and she kept her eyes to the floor. When she turned and walked away Bullet, being a man, couldn't help but notice the swell of her ass, even under the drape of the big skirt.

Hmmmmn, he thought. *That nigga Sugar may have something going on there. I wonder what the rest of her looks like.*

These thoughts brought him back to the situation at hand. Should he go through with the deal as he'd put it to Sugar? Or should he follow through on his own plans and cap him and these bitches? It was his option.

Trey and Brew wouldn't kill Sugar until he did the women. Farelli and the cops wouldn't come until he called. He could just get his money and leave. That would leave Jessica, Sugar, and Cole, all of whom in his opinion had disrespected him alive. The mousy one ahead of him didn't matter one way or another.

He wanted them dead. Especially Jessica. But that feeling of wrongness, of danger wouldn't go away. He wasn't used to that. Maybe he'd just let it play out. As long as he got his money back, he could live with the rest. If he could walk away from Jessica, he would. If not, he'd cap the ho.

Elnora stopped in front of a lit doorway on the right.

"In here."

The sight of Jessica sitting behind the desk sent a rush of conflicting emotion through him. So much so that a full minute had passed before he noticed that the other woman was gone. *Fuck it*, he thought. The little mouse could do what she would. If he killed Jessica and Sugar, she couldn't hurt him. He owned the cops.

Jessica. Damn, she looked good. For a moment he wished things were different. He'd love to be able to keep her. But no. Alana had been clear about what she'd said. Jessica, as well as the others, had been fucking Sugar all along. She'd handled him like a trick. His anger started to surface.

"Why?"

If he'd expected guilt and contrition, he was to be disappointed. She looked him square in the eye and didn't waver or flinch.

"Why? Can't you figure it out? For years I've been nothing to you but a pretty piece of pussy. Jump up and down on me for a few minutes, throw some money at me, then gone again.

"Every once in a while you'd take me around so you can show me off to your boys. And your women. Fucking any bitch that caught you eye. Trading dope for pussy. Coming home to me with their perfume on your clothes and their pussy juice still on you dick. You think I didn't know? Think I was a fool? People come over, treat me like I was nothing!

"You wanna know why I kept up my relationship with Sugar? He sees me. Really sees me. Treats me like a person, not just a piece of ass. He always did. If he loved me the way I wanted him to, I would have left you a long time ago. Why?"

Bullet was livid. The main source of energy fueling his rising rage was the knowledge that she was telling the truth. He, and all the men he hung with didn't allow women inside their feelings. They were to be used and enjoyed, then pushed aside until the next time the urge struck.

Just because she was right, though, didn't mean that Bullet was gonna cave in. He wasn't gonna fall weak for no woman like that nigga Sugar. As for the feelings he had for Jessica? He had ignored and denied them for so long, it was easy to do so now.

"You just like all the rest of them hoes. I ain't got time for this shit. Where the fuck is my money?"

Jessica rotated the monitor on her computer. The screen was split into two windows.

"On the left is your empty account in Antigua. On the right is Sugar's account. I hit a couple of keys and forty-seven million goes to your account. It's that easy. Where's Taneesha?"

"In the car out back. What are you waiting for? Put my money back."

"Bullet, I know you a lot better than Sugar and Cole. You're not gonna do right. Let Taneesha go to Sugar now. I'll give you your money. See Sugar's balance? He's got money, not forty-seven mil', but enough. We don't really need yours."

"Sugar! Sugar! I knew you was lyin' when you said you didn't love that nigga."

"I didn't say I didn't love him. I said he didn't love me. Sugar's not my man. Cole is. But as for Sugar, he's all the man any woman needs. I come every time I think about him touching me."

Just as Jessica had planned, that did it. Bullet was known for his insane rages. People often died when he went off. This time was no exception. He reached behind him for his gun as his other hand, fingers outstretched, grabbed across the desk for Jessica.

The 9 mm Baretta was only an inch from the back of his head when it went off. The front of Bullet's face blew out, spewing blood, bone, and bits of brains all over the desk and computer. Nora fired again into his body as it slumped off the desk onto the floor.

Chapter Forty-Eight

The AR-16 rifle Cole was using tonight had been fitted with a silencer. He had been on the restaurant's roof all along. When Bullet went inside after confronting Sugar, he rose to his knees. Pee-Wee never heard the shot that killed him.

Cole silently made his way to the other side of the roof. He removed the night vision scope from its mount and waited. The rear of the restaurant and the pit area was well lit. He could see Bullet's men at either end of the car.

Sugar still stood near the pit. His hands were casually hooked into his belt, but Cole knew it would only take a split second for him to raise and lower his favorite .45. He was tempted to kill these dudes and go get his woman.

He laughed to himself. Funny how everything could change in a matter of hours. Now it was him and somebody else. Cole the loner. Cole the killer. Who'd believe it? Well, he did. Sugar did. Who the fuck else had ever mattered to him? He was looking at part of the answer. Taneesha, Mary, Alana, and now Sugar's Elnora. Damn,

Taneesha sure was being real still. Maybe she was doped up.

The first shot was unexpected when it came from inside the restaurant. No matter. Cole's extraordinary reflexes and instant decision making were part of what made him so good at what he did. Almost instantly after the report he had put two bullets into Trey and was moving to the corner of the roof where a short length of rope lay.

Trey's body was flung across the hood of the Lexus with a *thump* as his knee hit the fender. This sound probably saved Sugar's life. Brew actually had his Uzi pointed in Sugar's general direction when the shot from inside came.

The sound of Trey hitting the car came immediately after. This noise caused Brew to whip his head around. Before he could find Sugar again the big .45 thundered. As big a man as Brew was, he was blown across the rear of the car as if he were weightless. Sugar was moving before his body hit the ground.

Cole had disappeared into the restaurant's interior when Sugar pulled the car door open. Taneesha was pale, her eyelids fluttering.

"Sugar?" Her voice was hoarse and weak.

"Sssh, baby. We got you."

Cole came out of the door, his arm around Jessica. Nora ran to Sugar.

"You okay, baby?"

"Yeah. What happened to Neesha?"

"She was shot already. Before she got here. Run get my truck."

"Will she be all right?"

"I don't know. Hurry!"

When Elnora slid to a stop next to the Lexus, Sugar lifted Taneesha and lay her on the rear seat.

"Take her to Gate Three. Tell the guard she's been shot.

Have him call Captain Farelli of the Biloxi Police. Since it's an emergency, they will treat her even if she's not military. Their trauma center is one of the best. You only know she was shot here and you tried to save her. Let Farelli straighten out the rest."

He was already on the phone when she tore away. After a short conversation, he gave Cole and Jessica a few directions on how to set the scene. The threat from Bullet was over, but they were still not out of the water yet. He walked over and picked up the Uzi near Brew's dead hand and loosed a few rounds toward the pits.

When Cole came out shortly after the sound of gunshots from inside, Sugar sent him away with instructions to wait for his call. Then he and Jessica went out front to wait for the cops.

CHAPTER FORTY-NINE

As he expected, Captain Farelli was the first to arrive. His unmarked car roared into the parking lot, dashboard light flashing and light screaming. With him was the same sergeant from the shooting at Sugar's house. Farelli jumped from the car, face tight, and rushed up to Sugar.

"Tell me about it."

"Bullet is dead in my office. There's a guy over by that Suburban, and two more around the back. That's it for here. Me and Jessica are the only ones still here. A friend of ours, Taneesha Shoals, was rushed to the Keesler Medical Center by my girl. They might call you about it. She was shot by Bullet or his people before they got here."

"They already called me. I told them to treat her and I would send over an officer to explain. Let's go inside and get this together."

The parking lot was filling with cars. The police cordoned off the lot, but the street beyond was overflowing with news vans and onlookers. Sugar, Jessica, and Captain Farelli sat at a table in a corner of the restaurant.

"Look, Captain, this shit is over. All that's left is damage control. The truth is, me and my friends were just defending ourselves against the jealous rage of a psychopathic drug dealer. I don't do or deal dope. None of my friends, including Cole, have anything to do with dope. I could just go out there and grab a reporter and tell the truth. That probably wouldn't be in everybody's best interest, though."

"Mr. White, you probably did the whole coast a public service by getting rid of Ollie and his crew. However, two dead at your house the other day, four dead tonight at your place of business, you can see that it's going to be a difficult, if not impossible, sell to keep you and your friends as non-participants in Ollie's business.

"Some things you may not know. Not only were Alana and Francisco De Leon killed, but also a drug dealer named Jesse Verdun and some of his people in Gulfport. Early this evening, more than twenty of Bullet's people were shot and killed. The last twenty-four hours have been a bloodbath around here. A real war. Somebody had to come up with some answers. That's me."

"Captain, I don't think either of us would be well served if the DEA, FBI, or any other law enforcement agency were to poke into this situation."

Farelli's eyes tightened. Sugar knew he had hit a sore point. The captain and most of his department were dirty. It wasn't exactly common knowledge, but the people in the know on the streets knew. And Sugar was aware that he absolutely had to have Farelli's cooperation for them to walk away from this. Being right didn't mean that he, Cole, and maybe even the girls weren't gonna go to jail.

The way he figured it, he hadn't just done the coast, but Farelli in particular, a favor. But for him, Cole, and their women, Bullet would have continued to roll until he drew both himself and the captain under the government's microscope. Plus there was the dirty cop's prime motivation. Greed. Farelli had been hedging his bets. He was gonna survive no matter who came out on top.

"Here's what I suggest, Captain Farelli. You give Jessica here your bank account number. I'm sure you have a hidden account somewhere. I do. She's going to transfer five million dollars into it right now."

The corners of Farelli's lips twitched, and Sugar knew he had him. It would take a long time to extort that kind of money in the usual payoff.

"You lay this whole thing, including all the shit from the past couple of days, off on a turf war between the drug dealers. Blacks against Puerto Rican. I'm only involved because my friend Jessica was Bullet's live-in girlfriend. When she discovered he was a criminal, she ran to me for help. The Ricans, unidentified of course, caught up with him and his men here. Me and Jessica were hiding and lucky to survive. Our friend Taneesha got shot in the crossfire. You'll have to explain the irregularities. Because the investigation is ongoing, we can't talk about it to the press. Cole doesn't come up."

"That's real close to what I had in mind. Minus the five million, of course. It's also close enough to the truth."

Farelli had removed a gold pen from his jacket. When he finished writing on a napkin, he handed the paper to Jessica. Without a word, she got up and left the room. When he was able to tear his eyes away from her ass, he looked back at Sugar.

"I'm going to do my part. You need to lay low for a while, and tell your friend not to kill anybody soon. You two have come a long way from The Strip. I had thought you got scared straight and had turned out to be a friendly sugar daddy. I was wrong."

"Kind of. It was all a game. I guess you could call it The Sugar Daddy's Game. In the world I grew up in, you learn that not everybody who walked through the whorehouse door was a real trick. But the game's over now."

Epilogue

Nora tapped lightly on the door. "Jessica, Cole, come on! They're here!"

Cole reluctantly let Jessica go. It had been a week since the shoot-out at Sugar's Bar-B-Q. He and Jessica had spent the better part of it locked up in this bedroom at Sugar's house. They had to come up for air now, though. Taneesha was coming. She had just been released from the hospital.

Mary and her husband, John, followed Taneesha through the front door just as Sugar and Shay came through from the kitchen. Nora, Cole, and Jessica stopped at the foot of the stairs. All eyes were on Neesha.

She looked good, if a few pounds lighter. Somehow, Farelli had convinced the base commander that her safety depended upon her being treated there until her release.

"What y'all looking at? I got a booger in my nose or something?"

That broke the tension. Everybody crowded around,

touching and kissing her, carefully avoiding the bulky bandage. Cole came last.

"Hey, baby. You okay?"

"Yeah. Hurts like a bitch, but I knew you and Sugar would come for me."

She noticed the way Jessica clung to Cole and raised an eyebrow. "So it's like that, huh? Good for you, girl. And who is this fine-ass bitch here? Tell me it ain't El-nora. I knew you was hidin' some real goodies under all that shit you wore. Sugar finally got you out of them granny drawers, huh?"

Everybody laughed.

"Who do you think figured out how to get your fine ass back in one piece?" Sugar remarked.

Shay pecked her on the cheek. "I still say you just a White girl who likes Black meat. You ain't foolin' me, girl."

"Speaking of Black meat, girl, they got a bunch of brothers on that base—doctors an' everything. Fine-ass niggas too. We got to go hunting for real!"

Mary sucked her teeth. "Right now your dead ass better hunt up a seat before you fall out. I ain't giving you another one of them pain pills for two more hours."

"Damn, Mary! Where your little rug rats anyway? I'll be glad when they take this shit off so you stop bossin' me around!"

They all filed into the living room and found seats. Sugar left and retuned with a stack of papers.

"We're going to eat in minute. I got some business we need to take care of . . ."

He handed a sheaf of papers to Mary.

"The restaurant now belongs to you, Taneesha, and Shay. Those are the deed transfers for it and this place. You can run it, sell it, or whatever. As long as you all agree. Jessica's got papers for a separate account for each of you. That money is yours. Me, Jessica, Cole, and Nora are leaving tomorrow. We'll stay a week in Belize to take care of some business."

Mary looked at him in bewilderment. "What you mean, Sugar?" You giving us the restaurant and the house? You're not coming back, are you? Is it because of . . . ?"

Sugar looked over at her husband a moment before he spoke. "No, Mary. It's not just because of The Game. That's over anyway. If we four stay here, there'll always be questions and people digging into what happened. Especially the Puerto Ricans.

"Me and Nora are moving up to Natchez. I got people there. Cole and Jessica are going with us for now, but you know Cole. We'll always have each other, always be family. But it's time."

The mood became sober. All the money in the world couldn't erase where they'd come from and what they had been to each other. The Game had been mostly a reflection of their desire to always be together, to never let go of the safety and security they had found in each other as children. Now it was time to grow up.

"Say, Sugar, they got any horny, big-dicked niggas in Natchez?"

"Shay, you got dick on the brain," Taneesha said.

"It ain't my brain that's itchin'!"

After the laughter died, Sugar spoke again. "While we're gone, I need you three girls to plan a ceremony. We're gonna have a double wedding on the Riverboat Casino Under-The-Hill in Natchez. We want you to set it up for us."

That brought on excited babble from all the women. Sugar smiled, then nodded at Cole and John. The three men left and let the women do what they did best. Be women.

About the Author

Greg Dixon was born and raised in Natchez, Mississippi. He attended college at Tuskeegee Institute. After eight years in the USAF (in Biloxi), he moved to Houston, Texas, where he now resides. Much of the material in his novels comes from a variety of real-life experiences and associations. Katina, Tara, Andrea, and AnnElisha are his daughters, and Gregory and Andre, his sons. He is currently working on his next novel, *King of Crack*.

SNEAK PREVIEW OF

King of Crack

BY GREGORY R. DIXON

Coming in Spring 2009

Prologue

Fuck! He was bleeding. He didn't think he'd been shot, but in the noise and confusion, he wasn't sure. Just like he wasn't sure they wouldn't come into the woods looking for him. At least they had stopped busting caps at him. Good thing, too, because his gun was empty.

That fucking Herman. He was dead, whether he knew it or not. One thing Big George had taught him early was that you didn't take disrespect from no man. The way he saw it, there wasn't much worse disrespect than trying to shoot a brother with no warning and no reason.

All he had been trying to do was sling a few stones,

make a few bucks to help out the old lady. Since Big
George got locked up, times were hard. These days, the
only way a nineteen-year-old brother with no job and no
real training could make any real money was the dope
game.

George King, a.k.a. Big George, was his daddy. He'd
gotten knocked off by the Feds over a year ago. Since
then, things had gotten rough for Chris and his Mama.
The Feds had frozen and confiscated their bank accounts.
When they got through snatching shit, all that had been
left was the old house on Lang Road that they used to
rent out, but lived in now, and the two cars which were,
like the house, in his Mama's name.

They had tried to take those, too, but George's
lawyer stopped them. Chris finished high school last
year. He played basketball and football and had started
in both. He was an okay high school athlete, but not
good enough to be recruited by the colleges. Since his
grades were average, there was no academic scholar-
ship.

The money George had put away for his college was
gone too. He'd tried, for his mama's sake, but with no
real skills except sports, he couldn't find a decent job. So
he had decided to help out in the only way he knew how.
Hustling. If dealing dope had been good enough for Big
George, then it was good enough for him.

It was Thursday night. He had been standing in The
Alley trying to get rid of his last bag of stones. When the
white Olds Ninety-Eight pulled in, he thought nothing of
it. He'd known it was Herman and two of his boys. They
were blasting 50 Cent, as usual. Chris just stood where he
was, in the shadows at the back of The Alley.

Halfway down the drive, the car stopped. Herman
killed the music and headlights. He got out, and BoBo
and Lee Arthur got down too.

"Hey, nigga! Where you at?"

Chris didn't know what they wanted, but he was the only one back here. "Yo. What's up?"

"Whatchoo doin' in my spot, boy?"

"What the fuck you talking about? You ain't got no spot. And I got yo' boy right here." He knew they couldn't see, but he grabbed his crotch anyway.

"I say this my spot, and you betta get to steppin', li'l nigga."

"Fuck you. My old man was dealing here when you was still shittin' yellow."

"Fuck me? No. Fuck you!"

The sound of the gun was like an explosion. The bullet ripped a chunk of bark off the tree to Chris's right. He pulled his nine and shot back. He was nervous and missed all three dudes. Herman, BoBo, and Lee Arthur all started shooting.

The bullets whistled past him. *Fuck*, he thought, *I'm dead.*

He started to move backward. There was a barbed-wire fence at the end of the street. Behind it were woods that stretched all the way to Bland. Chris misjudged the fence's position in the dark and ran right into it. He felt a sharp pain in his arm.

Diving through the fence, he hit the ground. It felt like his thigh was on fire, but he jumped up and ran. The shooting behind him had stopped, but he ignored the trail through the woods, and struck out through the undergrowth, forcing his way east.

His car was parked in Miss Jennings' yard over on Parkes Street, on the other side of Little York, opposite The Alley. He had more bullets there. The woods ended, and he saw he was next to the dirt yard, the rows of dump trucks lined up like soldiers. Looking to his left, he could see the lights of Drew Middle School.

Limping alongside the dirt yard fence, he made his way to Little York. He would have to cross the street and go about sixty yards up in order to get to Parkes and his ride. He was bleeding from the arm and the thigh. He stepped out into the street.

CHAPTER ONE

I stepped out onto the sidewalk and looked both ways up and down West Little York. To the right I could see the flashing light in front of the Fire Station, and beyond that, the traffic light at the West Montgomery. Left, the street was clear. I watched the entrance to The Alley, but it was empty.

Hobbling across the street, I turned left. This end of Parkes Street sat almost directly across from the entrance to The Alley. There were only four houses and a church on the street, and they were all on the right side. The left was bordered by a narrow strip of trees, then the school. The end had a short path through more trees, then the rest of the street, which dead-ended into Dolly Wright. I didn't see Herman's car, but there was a police car parked at the end of The Alley. A crowd was gathered.

I limped to Miss Jennings's driveway. The front of her house was dark. My car was pulled all the way around back. Usually, I gave her twenty or thirty dollars whenever I parked there. Bleeding, shook up, and with my gun in my hand, I decided to just leave and pay her to-

morrow. I had to get patched up and figure out a way to
kill those assholes who'd tried to do me. What I couldn't
figure out was *why* they'd done it.

I was really just getting started in the game. By working my ass off, I made a couple of grand a week. I didn't
have the old man's connect, so I bought wholesale from
this Mexican in Spring Branch and sold stones here in
Acres Home. It had been my Daddy's territory, so I knew
it well.

Just as I put the key into the car door, Miss Jennings's
back door opened.

"Psst! Psst! Chris. Come here! Come in. Quick!"

The light wasn't on, and though the voice was female,
it wasn't Miss Jennings.

"Who's that?"

"It's me. Jasmine."

"Okay. Be right there."

Jasmine was Miss Jennings's niece. We were kind of
friends, had known each other all our lives. I opened the
trunk, took out the box of bullets, and stumped up the
steps and into the house. A hand took mine.

"Come on."

She led me through the dark kitchen and into a bedroom. Closing the door, she fumbled around until a lamp
came on. Jas was five-six, with skin the color of a brown
paper bag. Her complexion was clear, and she had pretty
hazel eyes. God, she was fine! Big, full breasts, a narrow
waist, and ass for days.

"Jesus! You're bleeding!"

"Yeah. Somebody tried to cap me."

"It was that damn nigga Herman, wasn't it?"

"How did you know?"

"I'll tell you later. Sit in that chair. I will be right back."

As she turned to go, I asked, "Where is your aunt?"

"At my house with Mama." She left the room.

She came back with a big first-aid kit and some towels. That didn't surprise me, 'cause her aunt was the school nurse at Drew.

"I gotta boil some water. Take off your pants and shirt." She walked into the kitchen.

I've gotta admit, I was kinda nervous. I had always thought Jasmine was one of the prettiest girls I knew. We'd always talked and made eyes at each other, but nothing had ever come of it. We went to different schools, and I didn't live out here. Besides, when we were younger, both of us were too shy to make the first move.

Chuckling to myself, I thought, *Well, this ought to take care of the shy part*. I took off my pants and shirt and was standing there in my black boxers when she came back into the room with a bowl of hot water.

I could see her look me up and down before she said, "Sit."

It was okay while she cleaned out the cut on my arm from the fence. She washed it, poured in peroxide, smeared on a cream, and wrapped it in a gauze bandage. The trouble started when she got to the long gash on my thigh.

The wound was ugly and raw, but her hands were gentle as she cleaned it. Too gentle. My dick started to get hard, and wouldn't you know it, the damned thing popped through the opening in my shorts. Her eyes got big.

"Damn. That's a big one. I ain't no virgin or nothing, but I only seen a couple, and they was nowhere near that big."

Naturally, my head swelled with pride. She forgot about cleaning my wound, and reached out to touch it. That only made it harder. When she put her other hand on the crown, I jerked.

"Jas."

She came around and knelt between my legs. Working the shaft with both hands, she took the crown in her mouth. She bobbed her head up and down, sucking gently. It felt like heaven.

"Jas," I said again.

She raised her eyes, still sliding her mouth back and forth on me. Tightening her grip, she moved her head faster.

"I'm gonna shoot, Jas."

She just closed her lips tighter around my dick. I let go, lifting my ass off the chair, and she sucked me dry. I lay back, and barely noticed when she left. She came back into the room and cleaned me off with a washcloth. Her breath smelled like toothpaste. Wearing a self-satisfied smile, she went back to work on my leg.

I was shocked and trying not to show it. A lot of brothers had shot at her and gotten turned away. She wasn't no "ice queen" or nothing, but she had a way of making you feel that having her would cost more than you were willing to pay. As much as I had liked and admired her, it never occurred to me that she might be available. Especially to me.

"Hurry up and finish that so I can take care of you."

"Don't worry about me. You're hurt. You owe me one, though. First I got to figure out how I can take that thing."

"We'll work it out. Jas, why . . . I mean, what?"

"You mean why did I do that? Look, Chris, I don't mess around much. I am trying to find a job so I can maybe go to school." She wrapped my leg and tied off the bandage. Then she kissed me softly on the lips. "I've been wanting to do that since I was six years old."

"Tell me about Herman."

She did.

CHAPTER TWO

The house sat on Wilberforce Street between Sealy and Wheatly. The driveway was long and winding, ending at the carport of a small, gray, two-bedroom house. There were no other houses near on that side of the street. Several people kept horses on this end of Wilberforce, so a lot of the land was pasture. The house belonged to Herman Broussard. I was here to kill him.

Directly across the street from the driveway was an old orchard. The trees bore some figs, but the apples and pears were out of season. The foliage here was thick, though, and I waited. Jasmine would be calling the house any minute now. I couldn't see it from here, but I could see the end of the drive.

Why Jas was going so far to help me, I wasn't really sure, though I was glad. Maybe it was because she felt a little guilty about Herman trying to kill me. Maybe she cared. After today's work, I would know for sure. She'd be put to the test, but it was my ass that was really on the line. I hoped she was really as down as she seemed to be.

After she had bandaged me up last night, she told me

how Herman had been chasing her. She didn't like the dude. One of her friends had given him some play, and he had gotten her drunk and him and his two boys had all fucked her. He kept coming by Jasmine's house and giving her shit. Yesterday afternoon, when she was on her way to Miss Jennings's house, he had stopped her. She told him that when she left her aunt's house, she was coming over to The Alley to look for me.

I crouched down quickly among the fruit trees as headlights shone onto the road from the driveway. It was Herman's Ninety-Eight. He was on his way to pick up Jasmine. As soon as the tail lights disappeared up Sealy, I crept out of the trees. I was in a hurry because I needed to be inside the house when they got back. I knew it would be just him and Jas because she told him that she had heard about what had happened to her friend.

At the carport I pulled on my gloves. The backyard was fenced in, and I knew that he kept a pit bull. When I rattled the fence, the dog rushed around the house. I shot it three times. Jumping the fence, I poked it with my foot to make sure it was dead, then I dragged it under the house.

Kicking at the back door didn't do any good. It held solid. I busted out the glass in the kitchen window and climbed in. There was a huge bar set in brackets across the door. I walked through into the front room. There was a closet in the wall near the door. I stepped into it, pulled the door almost all the way closed, and waited. My hand was sweaty around the grip of my pistol.

It wasn't long before I heard the car coming. The headlights went out, and I could hear voices outside the door.

"Stop. Wait until I'm ready."

It was Jasmine's voice.

"I can't wait, baby," came Herman's gruff response. "I been waiting a long time. I gots to have me some of this."

Her laugh sounded forced. "At least wait until we get inside. I ain't one of your crackhead hoochie mamas."

Keys jangled at the door. I heard it open and close.

"Stop. Damn. You don't have to be so rough."

"You little bitch. You ain't seen rough. That ass is mines now. Think you too good for me? Well, if you is real good, maybe I won't call my boys like I tole 'em I would an' let them have a taste. Like we done yo' bitch friend, Linda."

I stepped out of the closet. "Maybe if you real good, I won't blow your little dick off and let my boys use you for pussy." I don't know why I was so mad. My hands were shaking with anger. Shit, I wasn't this pissed when the assholes shot at me.

Herman whirled at the sound of my voice. Jasmine stepped away from him. His hand whipped behind his back.

"Please try it. I'll cap yo' ho ass."

He brought both hands up, palms out. Anger and fear mingled on his face.

"Jas, get the gun out of his belt."

She pulled the automatic from behind him and cracked him hard on the head with the barrel before running over to stand by me. "Bitch-ass nigga, treat me like that."

As Herman grabbed his head, I looked at her and grinned. She definitely had spirit. I motioned toward the sofa.

"Sit down."

He went to the couch and sat.

"Take off all your clothes."

"What?"

"I said get naked, nigga. Don't make me have to say it again."

He stripped. Jasmine giggled.

"His li'l ole dick ain't half as big as yours."

I could see the anger and shame mount in his face. Another minute and he would do something stupid. I needed something from him before I finished it.

"Hush, baby," I said to Jas. "Where is your dope and your money? You and your flunkies tried to cap me last night. You owe me. I take your shit an' we even. Long as you don't fuck with my girl no more."

"Fuck you, nig—"

I shot him in the right leg. Jas jumped, and he screamed as blood shot from the wound. I had missed the kneecap and hit the shin bone.

"Next one's in your dick. Where?"

"Behind the dresser. Shit. You shot me. Behind the dresser."

I took his pistol from Jas and gave her mine. "If he moves at all, just point it and pull the trigger. Keep pulling it."

"I know how to shoot. I hope he moves. Killing this ho would be fun."

I ran to the big bedroom. The dude was sloppy. Clothes were everywhere. A big old-fashioned dresser with a mirror was standing against one wall. With an effort, I slid it out. In a hole cut into the sheetrock was a metal box about two feet square. I yanked it out.

Setting it down on the dresser, I flipped the catches and opened it. Two kilos of powder and a bread bag with ounce cookies were inside. I could see some green bundles of cash beneath the coke. I closed the box and turned to go.

On a hunch, I flipped up the mattress. Nothing. When I lifted the box springs, there was a covered shoe box wedged under the wire. Working it out, I took off the lid. It was full of cash. I went back up front.

Jasmine was holding the gun pointed at Herman, who was rocking back and forth in pain. Blood continued to pour out around his fingers. Handing the shoe box to Jasmine, I took the gun. Without hesitation, I shot Herman three times. Twice in the chest, and once in the head. Blood and bits of flesh flew. The stink of gunpowder filled the room.

Jasmine's face paled, but she didn't say anything. Placing the metal box on the floor, I put both guns in my belt. "Let's go. Did you touch anything in here?"

She shook her head. I picked up the box and we walked toward the door. Since Herman's house was isolated, I didn't think anybody would have heard the shots. If they did, they probably wouldn't have called the law, anyway. The fields and pastures around it were used for target practice by lots of people. I had even tried out my gun there when I bought it.

At the door I said, "Wait."

Pushing Jas out onto the porch, I set the box down again and went back in. I needed his cell phone. Finding it in his pants, I took it and put it in my pocket. Returning to Jas, I got the dope box and we walked away. Waiting at the last curve in the drive until there were no car lights in either direction, I hustled her across the street and into the orchard.

On the other side of the orchard, there was an old, abandoned house. My Lexus, or rather my old man's, was parked in front of it. Throwing the boxes in the trunk, we got in. I looked over at Jasmine. Her face was flushed, and she looked scared.

"You did good. Real good. We make a good team. And we got paid. Can you get away from home for a couple of days?"

"Why?"

"Because we ain't through yet. When we're done, I want you to come to my mama's with me. We'll chill for a minute. I'll be good."

She had to smile at that. "I guess so. What else do we have to do?"

I pulled out Herman's cell phone. "Here's the deal."

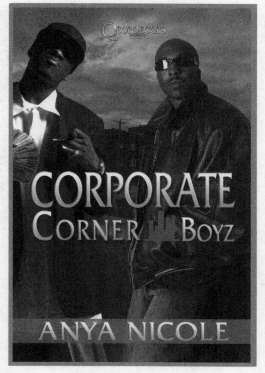

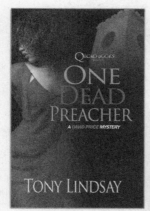

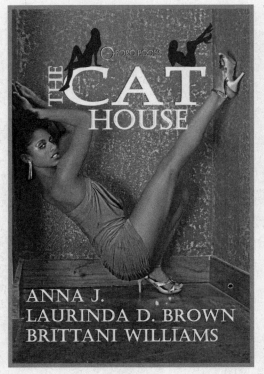